Like sparring partners they faced each other

Then Nicholas's eyes lost their coldness, a kind tolerant look replacing the steely hardness. His mouth relaxed into a smile.

"Despite all proof to the contrary, I fooled myself into believing you were a woman with normal needs. I believed that before the week was out, I would have you in my bed, that we would make love because we both wanted to, but I know now I was wrong." He ran a hand through the thick scrub of his hair and Victoria saw, as though watching from a dream, that his hand was trembling.

"You're safe, Victoria, so you may as well relax. No man wants to tangle with a woman who regards sex as something dirty and sordid and to be avoided at all cost...."

WELCOME
TO THE WONDERFUL WORLD
OF *Harlequin Romances*

Interesting, informative and entertaining,
each Harlequin Romance portrays an appealing
and original love story. With a varied array
of settings, we may lure you on an African safari,
to a quaint Welsh village, or an exotic Riviera
location—anywhere and everywhere that adventurous
men and women fall in love.

As publishers of Harlequin Romances, we're
extremely proud of our books. Since 1949,
Harlequin Enterprises has built its publishing
reputation on the solid base of quality and
originality. Our stories are the most popular
paperback romances sold in North America; every
month, six new titles are released and sold at
nearly every book-selling store in Canada and the
United States.

A free catalog listing all Harlequin Romances
can be yours by writing to the

HARLEQUIN READER SERVICE,
(In the U.S.) P.O. Box 52040, Phoenix, AZ 85072-2040
(In Canada) Stratford, Ontario, N5A 6W2

We sincerely hope you enjoy reading
this Harlequin Romance.

Yours truly,

THE PUBLISHERS
Harlequin Romances

Corporate Lady

Rosemary Badger

Harlequin Books

TORONTO • NEW YORK • LONDON
AMSTERDAM • PARIS • SYDNEY • HAMBURG
STOCKHOLM • ATHENS • TOKYO • MILAN

Original hardcover edition published in 1983
by Mills & Boon Limited

ISBN 0-373-02617-X

Harlequin Romance first edition May 1984

CHAPTER ONE

THREE days, she thought, three days stuck in this blasted resort with nothing but rain and more rain, and now . . . now that the sun has finally come out, he decides to sign the contract!

What a doddler! Surely by now he's memorised all the small print, she thought irritably, watching him study the pages one by one. She half turned in her chair to look out the window. The sun was still shining, but more dark clouds were looming. It would probably be raining by the time he had the darned thing signed.

She turned back to watch him and held her breath when it appeared he might pick up the pen. But no, he only pushed it farther away, a gesture over the past few days she had become accustomed to watching.

'Is there anything you're not sure of, Mr Harrington?' she asked patiently, wondering how many times she had repeated this question.

He glanced up, lines of misery etched plainly on his face making him appear much older than his thirty-odd years.

'No,' he answered bitterly, giving her a scathing look, 'everything is marked clearly right down to the last fork!' He picked up the pen and signed. 'I can't believe this has happened. I can't believe that someone can just walk in and take over someone else's property.'

She smiled and reached for the contract. 'I can assure you, Mr Harrington, that everything is quite legal, and if it will make you feel any better, my father has informed me that this is a very common business practice.' She folded the contract and placed it in her briefcase, taking out a cheque and handing it to him, 'Perhaps this will make you feel better, Mr Harrington,' she smiled.

He glanced at the cheque and tossed it on the desk. 'Your father is a crook, Miss Webster! I paid more than that as a deposit on this ranch!'

Victoria stood up and flicked back her long blonde hair, colour staining her pale cheeks. 'My father has a right to foreclose on your mortgage, Mr Harrington, and considering how you've allowed this place to become so run down, you're lucky to get that. Besides, that's only part payment, the rest will follow.'

'But this is prime real estate,' he argued. 'You must realise that prices have risen dramatically over the past few years in Northern Queensland, especially a holiday ranch so close to Cairns.'

'Oh, I wouldn't know about that, Mr Harrington,' she replied sweetly, locking her briefcase. 'I'm from Sydney, remember?'

The loud sound of a truck's motor prevented any further argument, and looking out of the window Victoria saw a horse float backing towards the main holding paddock. Mr Harrington left her standing by the window as he left the office, and soon she watched him walking towards the commotion the newly arrived horse was causing by refusing to back from the float.

She watched for a while, admiring the spirit of the horse, and then went to her room to put away her briefcase. Her encounter with Harrington had upset her and she lay down on her bed, her large grey eyes troubled as she stared unseeingly at the ceiling. As the newest and youngest recruit of her father's business, the Webster Corporation, she sincerely hoped that this would be her first and last takeover.

Judging from the frenzied sounds drifting through her

bedroom window the horse was still putting up a fight. She got up and sauntered over to her window, half hoping the animal would get away. Her eyes swept over the terrain, at the large patches of water that were starting to form on the flat of the land. She had heard rumours that flood conditions were starting to develop from the heavy rains, and now she could easily believe that such a possibility could come true.

She checked her watch, wishing she had booked an earlier flight back to Sydney. Damn that man Harrington for all his stalling!

She took a quick shower and changed into a pair of lightweight slacks and shirt. The horse had settled into his paddock and had been left alone, so she decided she would walk over and pay him a visit. He was handsome, she saw, black and beautifully shaped, far different from the mulish creatures Harrington housed in his stables.

She leaned over the rail and petted his nose. For a stallion he was docile, allowing her to grab his bridle and tickle behind his ears. Harrington came out of the stables looking as sullen and churlish as ever. 'Do you mind if I ride him?' Victoria asked. 'Does he belong to the ranch?'

'He belongs to a friend, and if you think you're good enough,' he shrugged, 'by all means take him out.'

He walked off, leaving her to stare after him. There had been a warning in his tone, and something else. A challenge, perhaps? She turned back to the horse. Maybe just a little ride around the enclosure of the paddock—there could be no harm in that, surely. She slipped over the top rail of the fence and swung her leg over the horse's back. There was no need for saddle and reins, she would only be riding for a few minutes.

The horse trotted nicely around the paddock. On the third round he gathered speed and flew over the rails, his feet barely touching the ground before he was off, travelling at breakneck speed. Victoria was aware of people running after them, shouting for her to stop. But she couldn't. All she could do was grimly hold on thinking at any moment she would surely be thrown off.

She was, but not until much later. Not until the horse had tired of her, rearing up to spill her unceremoniously to the ground, and then galloping madly away. Dazed and battered, Victoria got shakily to her feet, thankful at least that she was still alive. But she had no idea how far the horse had carried her or from which direction they had come. The waters had spread rapidly here and except for the occasional green tuft it was as though she was standing in a shallow lake.

She walked under the blazing hot sun, not realising that with every step she took she was heading further away from the ranch. As nightfall approached, bringing with it blessed relief from the heat, she dismally admitted she was lost. The waters were still rising and the clouds that had stood at bay now began to blot out the last blue of the sky. More rain was on the way.

She searched for a shelter and finally had to settle for a few rocks nestled against a clump of straggly old gum trees. She settled herself in, and not until the last rays of the sun had sunk below the horizon did she give up hope that she would be found.

By morning she was stiff and shivering from the cold, drenched to the skin from the intermittent showers that had fallen during the night. Never had she felt so miserable, and to make matters worse the water was now past her ankles, making walking a real hardship with the ground underneath sludgy and slippery.

There must be farms or homes somewhere about, she decided reasonably, but where were they? she wondered grimly as onward she trudged under the first dawning light. Finally she stopped to rest on a rock, searching the sky for the aircraft she had often read about who found people like her. And the search parties! Where was everybody? Surely Mr Harrington would have notified somebody that she was missing, lost, hurt?

As she watched the sky more rain began to fall, making her face the realisation that small aircraft would be unable to locate her with poor visibility, nor was it likely that search parties would know where to start looking for her, with the waters covering her trail. How long had she been listening to that sound? she wondered, before her numbed brain told her it was a motor.

A motor! A car? A truck? She half slipped from the rock and raced in the direction of the sound, her breath coming in tortured gasps as she stumbled through the water.

Past a clump of trees, she stood on a small clearing, and there it was below her. A road, or at least what was left of a road; it now looked like a canal. And travelling slowly along this passage was a jeep, headlights on and windshield wipers flapping. Victoria waved to win the driver's attention, but it was a useless exercise, she soon realised.

She was up too high, maybe twenty or thirty feet above the road. The driver of the jeep was obviously concentrating on his driving and not on the remote possibility that if he happened to look up he might see a tiny, fair-haired creature desperately trying to gain his attention.

She stepped closer and closer to the edge, jumping and waving her arms, her voice becoming hoarse as she called out. The ground had become weakened by so much rain and she didn't see the tiny pebbles and bits of dirt that were starting to roll down the side. She only felt the sensation of flying when the ground beneath her gave way and she was sent hurtling down the side to land in the path of the approaching vehicle.

When she awoke it was to find herself lying on a narrow cot with a patchwork quilt covering her, in some sort of shack. There was a table, a couple of chairs, a bench and two windows.

She could see that the rain had stopped and although the sun was shining, it felt damp and rather cool in the shack. Outside, someone was chopping wood, and she wondered uneasily who it was and how long she had been lying in such shabby surroundings.

Just then, the flimsy-looking door burst open and a giant of a man stepped through, his arms laden with wood. He cast Victoria a glance before kicking the door shut behind him, but he didn't speak until he had disposed of the wood by the fireplace. Well over six feet tall and powerfully built, his presence seemed to devour the space in the small shack.

As he approached her, she shrank into her pillows as though this small gesture might somehow give him more room.

'Well, Miss Victoria Webster,' he drawled in that unmistakable Queensland accent. 'Awake at last, I see, and in much better shape than you deserve to be. How do you feel?'

She plucked nervously at the quilt. 'As though I've been run over by a pack of mules,' she admitted with a grimace, rubbing the bump at the back of her head. 'B-But how do you know my name?'

He pulled a chair over to sit by the cot to gently, but thoroughly, examine the bump. 'You're a very lucky young lady,' he told her, studying her face. 'You might have been killed, but' apart from a few bumps and bruises you appear to be in perfect shape. As for your name,' he continued casually, clasping his hands behind his head and peering at her through narrowed lids, 'I happen to know that you're the young lady who robbed Teddy Harrington of his property and then stole a priceless stallion from his holding paddock, even though you knew the stallion didn't belong to Harrington but to a neighbour.'

'But that's not true!' she denied, her face registering shock at such a blatantly absurd accusation. 'I paid a fair price for Mr Harrington's property, considering how run down it was, and as for the horse—well, he said I could have a go on him, and I'm telling you, I wasn't on him for more than a minute before I guessed why. That beast is crazy, incapable of being controlled!'

'He wasn't meant to be controlled! He was a champion racer shipped all the way from Kentucky in the US and bought at a price that even you, Miss Moneybags, would find extravagant. He was meant for stud, to introduce a stronger breed of racehorse to Australia, but it seemed your impulsiveness and obvious disrespect of other people's property has most likely put an end to all that.'

He sat glaring at her, his eyes as black as the hair on his head. Through swollen lids, Victoria could see a muscle on the side of his jaw working spasmodically and the tight line of his lips told her better than words that this man despised her. Nervously, she brushed back the matted hair that had strayed across her cheek, stalling for time in a desperate bid to assess the situation.

'There seems to be some sort of misunderstanding,' she began, raising her hands and then dropping them in a hopeless gesture.

'Misunderstanding!' he snorted angrily a dark flush staining deeper the tanned hue of his skin. 'I'll have you know that while I was driving back from Harrington's I was thinking how if I ever met you I would cheerfully wring your neck! Just when my fantasies had stretched the limits of sanity, you floated across the path of my jeep. You can imagine my pleasure at finding the object of my fantasies floating helplessly into my arms!' He gave a low chuckle, before continuing. 'Lucky for you I came by when I did, otherwise you most certainly would have drowned.'

'Well, for goodness' sake,' she sparked, sitting upward in the cot, 'you needn't sound so cheerful about it! Anyway, I wouldn't have drowned. I saw your jeep approaching and I tried to get your attention, but I was up on the bank. The ground gave way beneath me and I fell. That's how I happened to be . . . floating, as you put it so charmingly, down the road.'

'So there you were and there I was, and now here we are,' he said with a malicious grin. 'Greed and theft and a flash flood have brought us together. It should prove interesting!'

'But if you knew who I was and where I was staying, why didn't you return me to Harrington's? I might have needed medical attention. Didn't you think of that?'

He smiled, but there was no humour in it. 'I examined you pretty thoroughly. Apart from sunburn and exposure, you were in one piece. The waters were rising steadily. I saw no advantage in risking getting bogged down on the way back to Harrington's, and not being able to get back up for a week or so myself. So,' he spread his hands to encompass the shack, 'I took you in and offered you the hospitality that Queenslanders are so famous for. I've made you welcome and trust you'll be comfortable for the duration of your stay.'

Victoria looked down at her hands clasped tightly on her lap and saw that they were trembling. She had the jitters—and no wonder! she thought with an involuntary shudder. The full realisation of her plight had finally struck home. She had been in grave danger and had narrowly escaped death. But that was over with, behind her now. Her main concern was that this man obviously considered that they were marooned in this tiny shack. The idea was unbearable, especially as he had undressed her; the loose-fitting man's shirt she was now wearing with nothing whatsoever underneath was undisputed proof of that fact. She felt stripped of her defences in more ways than one.

As though reading her mind, he indicated a large washbowl on a narrow bench which obviously was the kitchen section of the shack. 'I've left your clothes soaking. There's soap by the washstand. A good scrubbing should get rid of the mud.' He bent down and gently touched her cheek, a gesture so unexpected that tears sprang to her eyes. Brushing them quickly away, Victoria felt the need to offer some explanation.

But as easily as she had brushed away her tears, he brushed away her words. 'The swelling has gone down considerably,' he told her, his fingers continuing their probe. 'Even your eyes look much better.' He bent his head closer to peer into her eyes, while his hands cupped her face. For the first time in her life she wished she were beautiful. His nearness had an alarming effect on her and her heart beat so rapidly in her chest that she began to feel faint. She wondered what he would say if she told him now that this was the closest she had ever been to a man.

But of course she couldn't do that. His attention was purely clinical. Taking some eye-drops from a ledge over her bed, he made her lean back while he administered them. In a way it was a relief when it was over, because the drops afforded an excuse to hold her face in her hands and he couldn't have any way of knowing that the liquid streaming down her cheeks was salty and very much tasted of tears.

He took a clean cloth and patted her cheeks dry, and she pretended to study the bare wall in front of her. Then she felt a cooling salve being applied to her face, and the faint antiseptic odour she had noticed when she first awoke made her realise that this wasn't the first application of healing salve her swollen face had received. It also made her wonder how long she had been here receiving this wonderful attention.

She waited until the operation was over before asking. There didn't seem any point in distracting him. 'Have I been here long?' she ventured casually.

'A few hours,' he replied, placing the cap on the tube of cream, before placing it back on the ledge. Rising to his feet, he gave her a glance, but she noticed it was just to check the cream on her cheeks.

'A few hours?' she repeated in astonishment. 'But I thought . . . I mean, you indicated that I've been here for much longer than just a few hours!'

He glanced at the watch on his wrist. 'It's now ten past one. The first thing I did when we arrived here was send in a report to Harrington that you were alive and well. The time of that report was ten o'clock exactly, so, Miss Webster, you have been here exactly three hours and ten minutes. Now, if there are no further questions I'll get a fire started so we can have something to drink.'

His brusqueness offended her immensely but not nearly so much as the coldness in his voice when he addressed her, or the contempt in his eyes when he looked at her.

'Well, yes, actually, I do have a few questions, if you don't mind.' She waited to get his attention, for him to say 'What are your questions, Miss Webster?' or 'Fire away', or something like that. She didn't expect him to begin preparations for the fire as though he had suddenly forgotten she was in the room!

It was all too much. She swung her legs off the cot and took two faltering steps towards him. The sudden movement made her realise how weak she was and with a groan she felt for the cot behind her and gratefully sank down upon it. She decided it was best not to disturb him, to let him get on with the fire, and instead of questioning him she took the opportunity to study him.

She judged he was in his early thirties, maybe younger, though not by much. He was tall and ruggedly built, a welcome change from the fat and paunchy business associates that came into her sphere. With his thick black hair and long-lashed eyes, he was indeed extremely handsome. His casual clothes suited him—faded blue jeans which sat low on narrow hips emphasising the powerful length of well-muscled legs and a black T-shirt which enhanced broad shoulders and chest. His arms were bare, revealing a light covering of black hairs on his forearms. Deeply tanned, he made her feel pale and insipid by contrast.

When the fire was going he filled an old black kettle with water that he got from somewhere outside and hung it on a hook in the fireplace to boil. Wiping his hands on a towel, he turned to her. 'You have some questions you would like answered, Miss Webster?' He made it seem there hadn't been at least a fifteen-minute break in their conversation, but Victoria knew what his motive was. He was letting her know that he was in command here, not her. She had run into this sort of thing countless times in business. She sighed. Men were really such insecure creatures!

'Several, as a matter of fact,' she responded brusquely. A game was better if two were playing, she had decided. 'Question number one: How long will I be your '"guest"? Question number two: How did you get word to Mr Harrington that you'd found me? I don't see a telephone and I doubt we're within shouting distance of his place and yours.' This last bit was thrown in for humour, but one glance at his stony features told her he wasn't tuned in to her particular brand of wit. Undaunted, she continued. 'I resent unfair criticism when it's not justified—which leads to question number three. What business is it of yours that I should have a ride on that stallion, Dynamite or whatever his name happens to be. You hinted that he was worth a small fortune, so obviously he couldn't belong to you.' She allowed her eyes to wander aimlessly about the shack, leaving him no doubt of what she was thinking. 'Unless, of course,' she couldn't resist adding, 'you traded your kingdom for a horse.'

She had meant her words to be taken lightly, to throw some relief into their situation which was fast becoming unbearably tense. But obviously he considered her words fuel for fire, and the craggy features she had hoped to soften became even more brittle. His eyes narrowed dangerously and a deep flush spread across the dark hue of his skin.

'It doesn't surprise me, Miss Webster, that you would ridicule another man's lack of worldly goods.'

When Victoria started to protest, to defend herself, he merely raised a hand, and the gesture was enough to silence her. She decided then and there that she had never met a more despicable creature in all her life.

'Now, if you'll be quiet long enough I'll answer your questions. First of all, I think it best if you do not consider yourself my guest. As you've so discreetly pointed out, my residence hardly warrants such a gracious term. From this moment on you will be my partner, sharing equally in all chores for as long as we're here. Which will probably be anywhere from a week to ten days. The waters will have started to recede by then, making it possible for the jeep to traverse the roads.'

The kettle had come to the boil and he kept her waiting while he made some tea. He didn't ask whether she preferred coffee or what she liked in her tea. The cup he handed her was an old white enamel one, the handle unbearably hot. She juggled it for a while, willing herself not to spill the contents, but mercifully he retrieved the vessel from her hands and placed it with a thump on the floor beside her bare feet. There was no milk in the tea. Victoria hated tea without milk, but decided she would withold that information from him. She was aiming for pluses, not minuses.

Leaning against the fireplace with his ankles crossed and a cup in his hand, the man studied her in silence for what seemed an eternity. She knew what a picture she must present with her sunburnt and swollen face and eyelids, not to mention her scraggly hair and skinny legs hanging over the side of the cot. When she couldn't stand his penetrating gaze another second, she finally blurted: 'I don't think it's fair to stare at people, do you?'

She missed his smile because her head was bent in an effort to hide her embarrassment from him. 'Forgive me,' he answered softly, 'but I've never seen anyone quite like you before.'

Her head shot up. 'How dare you insult me!' she spluttered. 'I . . . I'll . . . I'll remember that!' She made it sound like a death sentence, which forced a chuckle from deep within his throat. He finished his cup of tea and crossed his arms, letting the cup dangle from his fingers.

'Your tea should be the right temperature by now,' he reminded her of the cup by her feet.

She shook her head. 'I hate tea without milk.'

'There's some condensed milk,' he offered. 'I'll get it for you.'

'No, that's even worse. Haven't you got any regular stuff?'

'Afraid not,' he said, coming towards her. 'The milk-man forgot to call today.' He picked the cup up from the floor and offered it to her. When she refused to accept it, he gave her a subtle warning. 'Either you drink this on your own, or I'll force you to drink it.'

Victoria accepted the cup and after a few sips decided that tea without milk wasn't really that bad after all. Especially when it was laced with plenty of sugar. While she was drinking, he dragged forth a chair from the small dining table, straddled it and with his arms folded across the top watched her in silence while she drank. She hadn't realised how thirsty she was or how a simple drink could offer such pleasure. When she had finished at last, he immediately raised himself from the chair and refilled her cup, scooping in plenty of sugar. 'The more you drink during the next few days the better off you'll be,' he told her as he passed her the cup. 'You weren't in the sun too long, as I understand you took Dynamite in the late afternoon. But even a few hours in the tropics can have devastating effects if one isn't prepared. It doesn't take long to become dehydrated.'

His tone had become conversational and although her sensitive ears could still detect a certain amount of coldness, most of the anger seemed to have disappeared. Most, but not all, and she was clever enough not to push her luck. For example, she would dearly have loved to point out that she hadn't taken Dynamite, that Dyna-mite had been offered to her, but she still believed that the less said about the horse the better. So instead she sipped at her tea and, as much as her swollen cheeks would permit, smiled at him over her cup.

The smile had no effect whatsoever. She could have saved her poor cheeks the effort, she decided gloomily as she finished the last of the tea and passed the empty cup to his outstretched hand. 'Thank you,' she murmured softly, once more feeling incredibly shy and awkward at his close proximity.

She watched his back as he carried the cup to the ledge by the washbasin that contained her soiled clothing, wishing she had complimented the tea out loud, told him how good it had tasted and how she had appreciated his effort of making the fire to boil the water so she could have some tea. That was what she might have said. Instead she heard herself asking in a voice that was far from pleasant and indeed a trifle too demanding for the occasion it warranted:

'Have you forgotten there are still two more questions that remain unanswered?'

Instead of being offended he was faintly amused. 'My, my, Miss Webster, the sun had a greater effect on you than I first realised! For a second you sounded like a spoilt brat. If the idea wasn't totally preposterous I might even venture to say you were trying to bully me.' His smile deepened. 'Perhaps you thought the same tactics for getting your own way would work on me the way they obviously did on poor Teddy Harrington.'

'Don't be ridiculous,' she managed through stiff lips. 'How could wanting a few answers be misconstrued as . . . as a carefully thought-out battle plan?'

His black eyes bored into hers. 'Yes, Miss Webster, how could it?' he parried. 'Shock tactics might work in the boardroom and a few other places, but they sure as hell won't work here.'

Victoria turned her head away. He was being unfair, but she didn't know how to rectify the situation, to make him more tolerant of her. Focusing her eyes on one of the patches that made up the patchwork quilt, she tried again, deliberately keeping her voice low and flat and void of any emotion that might be misconstrued.

'I don't wish to offend you, but if I'm to be here for any length of time I really can't see what there is to be gained by your constant reference to my business dealings with Mr Harrington. I also don't understand your connection with him or the horse. If you refuse to answer my questions, thereby robbing me of an opportunity of defending myself properly, then I don't think it's fair to be constantly badgering me.'

'And of course you like things done in a fair and orderly manner, don't you, Miss Webster?' he answered caustically, not sparing her a glance as he rinsed, dried and put away their tea mugs. 'But I can't remember saying that I refused to answer your questions. They're innocent enough to my ears—but perhaps you have ulterior motives for wanting additional information on Teddy Harrington.'

'Oh, for goodness sake!' she spluttered in frustration, glaring at him through swollen eyelids. 'Don't answer my questions if you don't want to! There's not much concerning Mr Harrington that I don't already know, and now that the deal has gone through, I have no further interest in him,' she explained reasonably.

'Like a vulture who has eaten its prey and has no use for the bones?' he asked, drawing a parallel. 'What did you do? Track down who was holding his mortgage?' he continued relentlessly, his black eyes never moving from her face.

'Now I know why you couldn't be bothered answering my questions,' she answered tersely. 'Obviously you had questions of your own.'

'And the answers,' he pointed out ruthlessly. 'You see, I already know how you purchased Teddy's mortgage and then tripled the interest rate. I know how you backed him so far into a corner that he had no hope of escape. Every cent he made went to the Webster Corporation, leaving him nothing left over for repairs and improvements. You bled him dry, leaving him no alternative other than to sell out at a price that must make you and your mob snicker up your sleeves. In case you can't understand what I'm driving at, Miss Webster,' he finished in a voice low with disgust, 'you didn't buy that property from Teddy Harrington. You stole it from him!'

Victoria smiled sweetly and tucked some loose strands of hair behind her ears. 'Ever since I joined my father's business, I've been up against your particular brand of ignorance. Most people are motivated by greed. Greed, and an inflated exaggeration of what their properties are worth, prompts them into thinking their holdings are more valuable than they actually are. If we didn't negotiate intelligently for each one of our acquisitions, if we paid top price for everything, we would end by having nothing. Only people who have nothing themselves tend to call us "thieves",' she added pointedly, 'others think of us as . . . shrewd.'

'A rose by any other name is still a rose,' he pointed out, ignoring her intended barb.

'And a leopard can't change his spots,' she retaliated angrily, 'no matter how much he tries, and I think you're trying too hard to prove something here that really isn't any of your concern. Unless of course I have something you want. Like Teddy Harrington's property?'

He laughed, his teeth sparkling white against the dark tan of his skin. 'A holiday resort would drive me mad in a very short space of time, I'm afraid. Besides, as you like to remind me, how could I possibly afford to buy such a place? Even the pittance you grabbed it for would probably be more than what's in my cookie jar,' he added, indicating a jar on the mantel with a few coins sitting in it.

Her cheeks blazed with colour that wasn't solely the result of her sunburn. 'I'm certain if you wanted it badly enough, you would find some way of getting the money. It wouldn't surprise me if you had pieces of eight stashed beneath the floorboards.'

'If I happen to find you prying the boards loose, I'll know what you're looking for,' was his smooth reply.

They glared at each other across the small expanse of the room and the air seemed charged with a kind of electrical current that crackled and rippled between them. Then suddenly the man smiled and stretched out his hand. 'Let's call a truce,' he invited gently. 'How about a guided tour of our little haven?'

But Victoria wasn't to be consoled so easily. 'Little is right!' she snapped. 'I feel like a moth that has been trapped and placed in a matchbox.'

'Interesting,' he drawled, 'that you should liken yourself to a moth instead of a . . . let's see . . .' he pretended to ponder, while making a show of studying her.

'I suppose you would have said a worm or a snake in the grass or something equally offensive,' she sniffed indignantly.

'No, oddly enough, I hadn't even considered those analogies, although I can understand why *you* might! For myself, I would liken you to a butterfly. Small, sensitive, fragile. A beautiful little butterfly . . . who's been taught to think of herself as a moth!'

CHAPTER TWO

THE compliment took her by surprise, leaving her with nothing to say. While a warm flush spread over her body, she chewed on her bottom lip, wondering if she should thank him.

It wasn't the first compliment she had received in the twenty years of her life, but it was definitely the nicest. Much better than: 'Your father should be very pleased with you this term, Victoria. You got straight A's; or 'You've earned your place in this corporation, Victoria, and that's why you'll become an equal partner. No one will dispute my decision once they learn that you graduated with honours in all your subjects. A son couldn't have done better. I'm very pleased.'

She smoothed the front of her shirt, her hands running lightly over the contours of her body, and suddenly her form took on a new status. She would no longer consider herself thin and scrawny. She was fragile . . . delicate . . . beautiful.

'I don't even know your name,' she told him in a kind of breathless wonder, as if he had proposed to her instead of just paid her a compliment.

'Nicholas Sangster,' he introduced himself with as much aplomb as if he was telling her the sky was blue. 'Ready for your guided tour now?' he asked as he opened the door, leading on to a large and airy breezeway.

Two sides of the breezeway were screened, while one well housed various cooking utensils. A long pine bench ran across the wall and on top of this was a small portable gas stove, a hurricane lantern, a tin box with the word 'matches' scrawled across the top, and farther down the bench was a pile of magazines that looked yellow and old. Below the bench were several stools, all painted red.

Next to the bench stood a large old hutch with screened doors. Victoria could see crockery inside, plates, cups and several bowls. Next to the hutch was a set of bunk-beds that looked as though they might have been hand-made. The same brightly coloured patchwork quilts lay on these as on the cot she had rested on.

Against one of the screened-in walls was a round dining table of scrubbed pine. In the centure of this was a large wooden bowl laden with fresh tropical Queensland fruit. This room, except for the two screened-in walls, was similar to the first room, perhaps a bit larger, but with the same sparse furnishings. Both rooms were purely functional, but Victoria was gazing through rose-coloured glasses, and this room became the most beautiful room she had ever seen.

She spread her hands across the screens to gaze at the frangipani trees that were pressing against the enclosure, and her small straight nose wrinkled as she sniffed at the delightful fragrance of the red, white and pink blossoms. Sunlight filtered through the sprawling green leaves, casting shadows across her cheeks. In the oversized white shirt hanging loosely on her slender body, she resembled a hungry waif staring at the goodies in a sweetshop.

Nicholas Sangster crossed over and stood beside her, his eyes searching her face for clues that might give credibility to the harsh account of her character given by his good friend Teddy. A flock of budgerigars, green and yellow, swooped down to rest on the branches of the trees, and their sudden appearance, accompanied by their screeching noise, startled her, making her draw back in alarm.

Nicholas Sangster grinned and placed a reassuring arm around her shoulders. 'Nothing to fear from them,' he laughed, 'unless of course you have sensitive ears. They can be overpowering in a group.'

With an arm still around her shoulders, he reached with the other to slide aside part of the screening that served as a door. Once outside he pointed out where she could safely walk on boards that had been stretched across the muddy red soil.

'You'll have no trouble if you keep on the paths,' he explained. 'Even though the flood waters will never reach us, the rains have made the ground very muddy.'

Victoria nodded her understanding and then proceeded to follow him as he led her away from the shack and towards a lean-to that sheltered the mud-encrusted jeep. Opening the door, he helped her inside and then followed her, swinging easily into the space she vacated as she scrambled towards the other side. 'Do you know what this is?' he asked, tapping a rectangular box below the dashboard.

'It looks like a radio,' she answered, studying it closely.

'That's what it is,' he said, 'but it's no ordinary radio. Have you heard of CB or Citizen's Band radios?'

'Yes, I have,' she acknowledged, bending forward to study it better, 'but I've never seen one.'

She watched with interest as he turned and twisted a few dials. Voices came over the air, each with his or her own code name, and he in turn gave his. Victoria laughed when she heard him identify himself as Black Angel, and then found herself listening attentively while he spoke to Tomahawk. When he had finished and turned off the receiver, he turned towards her. 'As you've probably guessed, you're Fallen Doe and it was Teddy Harrington that I was speaking with. I've let him know that you're fine and that he should notify your father, Sly Fox, that you'll be back in Sydney probably by the end of next week. I hope you don't object to the names we've given you and your father, but as many ears would have been tuned into our conversation, it's best to keep your identities secret. Once you're out of here, no one ever needs to know that Fallen Doe was really Miss Victoria Webster, daughter of millionaire Malcolm Webster.'

'But why should I care if anybody knows? I haven't kept my visit to Harrington's a secret. No matter what you think, my dealings with Harrington have been on the level.'

'I'm not talking about the deal between you and Harrington,' he answered patiently. 'What I'm talking about is your reputation and how it would seem to others if they knew that the daughter of one of Sydney's most prominent business men spent a week unchaperoned in a small, secluded spot above Cairns, in the sole company of one Nicholas Sangster. The gossips would have a field day with that little bit of news, now wouldn't they?'

'I can't see why,' she answered innocently. 'I was lost and injured and you rescued me. You said before that strangers to the area can get bogged down during the floods. I've read in the newspapers about such things happening, so it's not as though I'm the first person who's ever run into difficulties during a flash flood, as you called it. People will look on you as a hero. I know my father will,' she finished shyly, wondering at the strange, disbelieving look he was giving her.

'You don't think people will speculate about our activities during the long, lonely days and nights?' he asked with a slightly mocking smile. 'You don't think people will add two and two and come to their own conclusions?'

'So what if they do?' she answered evenly. 'I can handle it, even if you can't. I've been up against rumours and speculation all my life. You're not forgetting, surely, that you've condemned me on the basis of rumour. I haven't suffered a breakdown over that, and I certainly wasn't shamed into promising to offer Teddy Harrington back his property. Besides,' she laughed gaily, eyes twinkling, 'it might even be good for business. People might flock from miles around to view the place where Fallen Doe fell victim to the advances of the notorious Black Angel. We could set up a shrine and have guided tours. The guests would all stay at my new resort, of course, and every now and then . . . say Saturday nights, I could put in a special guest appearance. Perhaps as a special treat,' she finished mischievously, 'you could accompany me.'

He laughed and reached over to tossle her hair. 'You're a little vixen, not to mention an opportunist. As long as you make certain you don't include me in any of your shenanigans, it should be entertaining to watch your progress. However, a shrine is definitely out. I like my privacy too much. But I'm glad about one thing,' he went on, suddenly serious, 'that you won't be taking any gossip concerning us too seriously. I certainly wouldn't want to be the cause of any friction between you and your business associates.' His tone was light, but there was sarcasm in his voice.

Reaching behind him to the back of the jeep, he produced an old grey and grease-stained hat, which he made certain shaded her face adequately before they continued on the rest of their tour.

'I know what that is,' laughed Victoria pointing to the outhouse. 'It's a thunder box. I've never seen one before, in fact all this is new to me—those water tanks over there, the henhouse, the woodpile, those crazy little windows in your house. I feel really excited,' she told him, her face glowing. 'I feel as though something wonderful has happened to me. Have you ever felt like that?' she implored, as though seeking some sort of confirmation about her own feelings, that what she was feeling did indeed exist and that others had felt it, too.

They had stopped to rest under the shade of a huge old fiddlewood tree, its white conelike blossoms surrounding them with a fragrance similar to sweet jasmine. Victoria was sitting on the ground, her arms clasped around her knees, her head resting against the gnarled old trunk. Nicholas Sangster was standing next to her, leaning casually against the tree, long fingers hooked into the belt loops of his jeans.

'Yes, I've had that feeling,' he answered softly, not looking at her but at the fenced paddocks just beyond where they rested. 'I had that feeling when Dynamite was purchased, and again while I drove down to Harrington's to collect him.'

'Oh!' she replied in a barely audible voice, wishing with all her being that she had never introduced the topic of feelings. 'I'm sorry about Dynamite and his disappearance—I truly am,' she continued, rising to her feet and tugging gently at his arm to gain his attention. The hat which was many sizes too large for her partially hid her eyes, so that she was forced to tilt her head way back in order to look up into his face.

When he turned towards her, he half smiled as he plucked the hat from her head and hid her face with it, before returning it to its rightful position. Then he took her arm and led her back to the shack. Once inside, Victoria flung the hat on to the counter bench and then flopped wearily on to a chair, while Nicholas Sangster began preparations for a rather late luncheon. She watched absently while he opened a tin of mushroom soup and heated it in a saucepan over the gas burner. After spreading butter and jam on thick slices of bread, he placed these on a platter along with some buttered scones. Neither spoke until the soup was ladled out, eaten and the bread and scones had disappeared, and then it was Victoria who broke the silence.

'You ignored my apology,' she said softly, a faint tremor in her voice threatening to expose the deep hurt she was feeling. 'Despite what you think, I am truly sorry that Dynamite hasn't been found. I heard Mr Harrington telling you that the Air Rescue Service were keeping an eye out for him while they searched for flood victims. Besides,' she added on a false note of cheerfulness, 'he hasn't been missing for long, not even for twenty-four hours. He's probably having an innocent romp somewhere, enjoying his freedom.'

'Valuable racehorses aren't supposed to romp through scrub or flood waters,' Nicholas replied sarcastically. 'If he injured a leg when he stumbled while you were riding him, he could be bogged down in mud more treacherous than quicksand. If he didn't hurt himself,' he continued relentlessly, 'then he will most certainly come down with pneumonia. Racehorses are extremely sensitive creatures and without the care they deserve, they can easily fall prey to any number of diseases.'

'I happen to know a little about horses myself,' she volunteered recklessly, 'although obviously you consider yourself to be the only authority on the subject. It might interest you to know that my father and I have several racehorses and all of them have done extremely well on the track,' she finished proudly.

'If I ever get Dynamite back, I'll make certain that none of his progeny are racing against Webster stock. I believe in winning fair and square!' he commented drily.

Victoria couldn't believe her ears. 'What?' she gasped, rising to her feet and holding on to the edge of the table with hands that were trembling. 'Are you insinuating what I *think* you're insinuating?'

He leaned casually back in his chair, hands clasped behind his head. 'Now what could I possibly be insinuating, Miss Webster?' he drawled softly.

'You know damned well,' she said, fighting to hold back tears. She hadn't cried since she was practically a baby, but this wretched man seemed capable of making her cry at a drop of a hat. 'You said . . . you hinted that the Websters are involved in *fixing* races. That's a terrible accusation to make of anyone, and . . . and I demand an apology!'

Nicholas leaned forward in his chair, his tanned and muscular arms folded across the table. 'Apologise, Miss Webster?' he asked softly, dark eyes glittering. 'For what, may I ask? I never used the word "fixed". You supplied that one all by yourself.'

'Of course I did, because you put the word in my mouth,' she replied, anger and frustration replacing the hurt and disbelief she had felt. 'I don't think I should have to put up with your slanderous remarks any longer. There must be some way of getting me out of this rotten place,' she added, looking away from his smouldering eyes and quite forgetting that only an hour or so ago she had thought everything quite beautiful. 'What about one of those light aircraft that are used to rescue people? I'm a flood victim, aren't I? Well, I demand that you contact somebody to get me out of here immediately!'

'Can't be done,' he said, shaking his head and watching her now with amusement. 'Air Rescue Service is only used for extreme emergencies, and as long as you've got food and shelter you would not be considered an emergency.'

Victoria crossed the room to gaze out the window, unable to bear the smug look on his face any longer. 'There's no possible way out, then?' she asked in a voice heavy with despair.

'None whatsoever,' she heard him drawl.

'You're enjoying this, aren't you?' she accused him, as she turned from the window to gaze at him. 'You like having me here as your prisoner, being forced to listen to your jealous remarks about me and my father, in fact the whole Webster Corporation. You haven't stopped attacking me since I opened my eyes. You're playing a game with me, aren't you?' she accused through narrowed and suspicious eyes, as a new thought occurred to her. 'When you think perhaps you've gone a little too far, you retreat, play up to me by offering false compliments, calling me a . . . a . . . butterfly instead of a moth,' she stammered, feeling her cheeks burn with shame as she remembered how pleased his words had made her. 'Then outside, cautioning me to stay on the boards so I wouldn't get stuck in the mud, or fall, or . . . or anything,' she finished lamely, unable to continue against the steady black gaze of his eyes as they seemed to bore into her.

'My dear Miss Webster,' he said with exaggerated innocence, 'are you insinuating what I *think* you're insinuating?'

'Yes, I am,' she snapped, refusing to be baited by having her own words flung back at her. Along with his other false notions regarding her, he must think she was dumb as well, she thought disparagingly. 'Now that I know what you're up to, it shouldn't be much fun for you to continue your charade, so why don't you just get off my back?'

'I wonder if Teddy was as upset as you obviously are now, when you were riding his back?' Nicholas asked her quietly, black eyes narrowed as he watched her closely. Like a cat watching a mouse, thought Victoria, as she fought to keep her gaze from wavering from his eyes. She wasn't about to give him the satisfaction of appearing to flinch, as though indeed she might have something to feel guilty about.

'It wasn't necessary to ride Teddy's back, because I came equipped with facts and figures,' she replied in even tones. 'It is not the Webster policy to browbeat people into giving us what we're after, although it certainly seems to be the Sangsters' policy.'

'If I didn't know better, it would almost appear as though you did Teddy a favour by relieving him of his property,' he answered casually.

Victoria eyed him warily. What game was he up to now? she wondered suspiciously. 'I wouldn't be so bold as to answer for your good friend Mr Harrington,' she answered casually, 'but I think it would be safe to assume that his guests would think that we had done *them* a favour.'

One black brow shot up. 'Suspicion based on assumption, Miss Webster? That doesn't sound like good business to me.'

There was an arrogance in his tone that made her want to lash out at him, to strip that annoying smugness from his handsome features. But years of careful training came to her aid and she was able to present an appearance of outward calm as she smiled sweetly and said: 'Now really, Mr Sangster, what could *you* possibly know about "good business"? I daresay that you and Teddy Harrington are in the same league, but then,' she stifled a yawn, 'we can't all be successful, I suppose. The world is a big place. It can tolerate its social drop-outs, its misfits, the ignorant and the arrogant.'

If her intended barbs had any effect on him, it was only to give her the impression that he thought she had taken leave of her senses. She would have to sharpen her arrows if she hoped to penetrate his tough skin, she decided wryly, without asking herself why his destruction was so important to her.

'I think you've somehow lost track of our discussion Miss Webster,' he suggested, as though she were suffering from a bout of senility. 'Surely you remember we were discussing Teddy's guests?'

Damn him! 'Yes, well . . . I decided against pursuing that particular subject. After all, they're my guests now, or rather they will be as soon as all the legal work has been completed. And as you seem to detest anything and anybody that has connections, however remote, with the Webster Corporation, I kindheartedly decided against reminiscing over my guests.'

He laughed and pushed back his chair, getting to his feet. 'Oh, I don't think anyone would ever accuse you of being kindhearted, Miss Webster,' he drawled with a mocking smile. 'Not when there are so many more suitable words to adequately describe you with.'

'You've already tried that line with me,' she reminded him coldly. 'It's going to be one hell of a boring week if you insist on repeating yourself.'

'But I still say you're not a moth,' he said, coming towards her and crooking a finger under her chin. 'No, definitely not a moth,' he repeated, as she began to squirm under his penetrating gaze.

His hand left her chin to wander aimlessly down her slender throat. Victoria swallowed hard and shut her eyes, trying to ignore the clamouring of her heartbeats.

'Suddenly at a loss for words, Miss Webster?' asked

Nicholas as his hand circled her throat and worked its way into the tangled mass of blonde hair.

'Let me go!' she protested, forcing herself to open her eyes, only to be blasted with the full potent power of his own dark ones. He merely smiled—a smile that told her he *knew* she didn't want him to let go. This enraged her more than any other action could have. When his hand moved from her hair to trace the delicate outline of one little ear, she pulled her head back, pushed hard against his chest and practically screamed: 'Didn't you hear me, you country bumpkin, I said to let go of me!'

Ignoring both her words and her actions, his hands continued their assault, while his eyes remained on her face, watchful, intent, as though to determine how far he could torture her before she became quite mad. Slowly he bent his head, his eyes finally leaving hers to rest on her lips. 'No!' she gasped, realising his intent and trying to twist away from him. But his arms had encircled her, forcing her against him, and despite her struggles to free herself he explored her mouth as thoroughly as if she had been a passive recipient in his arms instead of the outraged wildcat she really was.

'Not bad,' he drawled with a triumphant smirk when he finally released her. 'Of course, along with anything else, the more practice you put into a thing the better it becomes. Perhaps that's how we can overcome the boredom you seem to fear. We can kill time by teaching you how to respond to a man instead of thinking of him as an enemy. Who knows,' he continued in a voice that was soft and therefore more dangerous because of it, 'by the end of your stay you may be convinced that you are, after all, only a woman!'

Trembling from the effects of having his hands roam over her body as though he, and not herself, owned it and the pressure of his lips still felt by a fiery tingling sensation, Victoria knew his words carried a warning that was more than a threat. She had no doubt that this man was capable of seducing her and possibly even managing to tear down all the carefully constructed barriers that had been designed by her father to protect her from just such a fall. She was on the threshold of a career that had, in actual fact, begun on the day of her birth. Her life had followed a carefully laid out plan, and this plan did not include becoming involved with a man, any man. Men were dangerous creatures, capable of malicious assault on a woman's emotions, robbing them of any opportunity of competing in a man's world. She didn't want that and her father didn't want that, any more than he wanted a son-in-law taking over his business. Victoria's mind was whirling, making her confused. She had thought herself incapable of ever feeling anything more than friendship for a man. Practically every man she had dated had bored her sufficiently to prevent her from accepting a second date. Others she had endured until it became too painful for her to bother, and then she had left it to her father to get rid of them. But this man Nicholas Sangster had affected her in a way she had never suspected possible. He made her *want* to be beautiful, while his mere touch sent her pulses racing. He had made tears come to her eyes and he had goaded her into ridiculously fruitless arguments. She had been happy when he was showing her around his premises, as though the harshly beautiful landscape was more than she could possibly compete with, and she had been willing to allow it to dominate her, and this had brought a feeling of peace into her being. And now . . . now he had kissed her, caressed her, and by so doing he had awakened in her all that her father had warned her against. She felt she was not beautiful, that in no way could she possibly be described as voluptuous, and that this man was far too handsome and virile to be interested in the likes of her.

It could only mean one thing. He wanted what was hers. He wanted her wealth and the power that went with it. He wanted her father's empire. Feeling sick to her stomach, she pushed past him and went to stand by the screened enclosures in the breezeway. She heard him moving about in the small room she had just left and she could tell by the sounds that he was getting ready to light the fire. That meant he would be coming out to go to the woodpile, and she didn't want to be near the door that he would have to use.

Quickly she skirted over to the other side, banging her ankle on one of the red stools and causing it to fall over. Just as she was rubbing her ankle and trying to right the stool all in the same movement, Nicholas opened the door and stood watching her.

'Well, don't just stand there gawking at me,' she snapped, 'd-do s-something!'

'What would you like me to do?' he asked, and there was no mistaking the amused mockery in his voice.

'Get me out of here, that's what. I don't believe for a minute that it's an impossibility,' she managed to gasp through clenched teeth as she rubbed her poor ankle, while hopping over to one of the more accommodating chairs.

Nicholas leaned against the door watching her as though she were putting on a comedy solely for his benefit. Then he went over and knelt in front of her, taking the small and slender foot in one of his big tanned hands. With the other, he stroked the slightly reddened ankle and then announced in a deadly serious taunt: 'Your ankle is fine, Miss Webster, nothing to moan about. It's just one of life's little knocks to remind us that we're . . . human, and that we mustn't take ourselves too seriously.'

Victoria wrenched her ankle free and tucked it under her shirt. 'Don't touch me, ever again! You're barking up the wrong tree, Mr Sangster, if you think you can have your way with me. I can't be bought and I won't be sold . . . to you, or to anyone. And I want out of here. *Now*!'

He leaned on his haunches, hands resting lightly on his knees. 'I'm sorry, Miss Webster, I really am, that I can't make good your request. I'm not enjoying your company any more than you're apparently enjoying mine, but I can appreciate your impatience. I realise there must be more deals to make, more hearts to break, more money to be had. But just this once your polite little request to leave must be thwarted. I'll repeat just once more and then I'll expect you not to ask again . . . there is no way out of here and there won't be for at least a week. You can sulk and cry and gnash your teeth, or do whatever you do when you don't get your own way, but it will all be to no avail. We're stuck with each other whether we like it or not, so we may as well make the most of it.'

'And is that what you intend doing, Mr Sangster? Make the most of it?' she asked in a voice that was loaded with bitter sarcasm. 'Do you intend forcing me into some sordid relationship that neither of us wants just so you can collect a ransom at the end? Because if you are, my dear fellow, I can spare you the effort by telling you it won't work.'

'Now what are we discussing . . . I'm afraid you lost me somewhere between this room and the other.'

'Don't pretend you don't know what I'm talking about,' she ground out. 'My father has warned me time

and time again about your particular brand of blackmail.'

'Blackmail!' he barked incredulously, running a hand
through his thick black hair. 'What's wrong with you
anyway?' he growled, grabbing her shoulders and shaking her. 'I've taken steps, as you already know, to
prevent anyone ever knowing that you were here. If
you're worried about your father, you needn't be. The
only person who would tell him about your stay with me
is yourself, and whether or not you decide to do that is
your own business.'

'I don't believe you,' she said in a low voice. 'Naturally
you'd try to lull me into a false sense of security to gain
my confidence. You've already tried flattery and when
that didn't get you anywhere you decided a little lovemaking would do the trick. Since I didn't respond to *that*,
I'm certain you intend using other ploys to make me . . .
fall for you.'

'After I've spent the whole week racking my brains
to dream up new and wondrous ways to make this
phenomenon a reality, what do I receive at the end?' he
asked softly. 'I can't wait to hear the bottom line.'

'As though you didn't know,' she answered bitterly. 'I
bet you've done this sort of thing to countless other
women.'

'Oh, I have, I have,' he agreed, reaching out to stroke
her hair, 'but as luck would have it, I've never had one as
rich as you. Come on,' he coaxed, tracing the outline of
her ear. 'Will he pay me off, your father, in gold or
silver, or does he prefer unmarked bills? Or perhaps his
speciality is a one-way ticket to oblivion. Or will he try
ruining me—you know, take away my little homestead,
my chooks, my muddy old jeep? Or does he only get
really nasty if a bloke refuses to be bought? What does
he do then, Victoria, does he have them beaten up,

thrown in the river? But then I suppose he hasn't had much opportunity for that kind of sport. After all, you're very young, there couldn't have been many men in your life.'

'I'm positive he would do whatever he deemed necessary,' she replied coolly, jumping up from the chair and away from his hand that was becoming dangerously enticing.

'You can forgive my curiosity when I ask what happened to the girl who thought it amusing that anyone would speculate about our predictament. Am I to understand the guided tours and the shrine is out?'

'Laugh if you want,' she told him fiercely, 'but that seems another life away. That was before . . . before . . .' She couldn't finish, couldn't say aloud what was on her mind, in her heart.

'Before I kissed you?' Nicholas volunteered wickedly. She swung away, refusing to meet the challenge in his eyes.

'N-No, of course not. What's in a kiss, for goodness' sake, do you think I haven't been kissed before?'

'I *know* you haven't been kissed before,' he replied coolly, 'at least not properly.'

'And that . . . that disgusting and barbaric display of calisthenics was a kiss? A *proper* kiss?' she blazed.

Ignoring her question, he continued to probe. 'So it's permissible if I flatter you, that didn't cause much of a commotion, although I strongly suspect you were . . . er . . . secretly pleased,' he said, chuckling at the sudden height of colour in her cheeks. 'No, it was the kiss that did it. It jarred you more than it should have.'

'It jarred me all right, but not in the way you hoped,' Victoria flashed back at him. 'At the risk of upsetting your ego, Nicholas Sangster, I found your kiss repulsive, distasteful, and it makes my stomach sick every time I think of it . . . *and* the way your hands pawed my body. Does that hurt your feelings?' she enquired triumphantly.

'Not in the least, but I would question why you torture yourself by thinking of it so often if it makes you ill?' he returned innocently.

'Ooh!' she ejaculated in a long-drawn-out note of frustration. 'Must you put a double meaning on everything I say?'

'As you're the one who refuses to accept things at face value, I'm surprised you object to, shall we say, a *form* of double-talk?'

'Now what's *that* supposed to mean?' she asked.

'Well,' he drawled, 'I've never spoken to a computer before, at least not a human computer, so I'm trying you out, testing to see which form of communication gets the best results.'

Her mouth fell open in shocked surprise. 'A computer?' she queried blankly.

'Well, I could be wrong,' he rebuked himself, 'but it has occurred to me several times today that you're a person who's been programmed to perform against your basic character. Now hear me out,' he admonished when she began to protest, 'I've known you just a short while, but already I've seen glimpses of the real Victoria Webster, the girl she would be, or would have become, had she been allowed.' He studied her for a moment before continuing, as though he wanted to be sure of how far he should go. Then with an impatient shrug he continued: 'For instance, have you ever had a friend, I mean a real, "just us girls together" kind of friend? How many dreams or hopes were you allowed before they were squashed? What about toys when you were a kid? I'll bet they were games like Monopoly and chess and very little else, or perhaps your toys were all at Daddy's office where you watched the real thing.'

Victoria clamped her hands over her ears and shouted, 'Shut up, do you hear me? I will not tolerate any more of your insulting lies!'

With the ease of a leopard Nicholas crossed the room and snatched her hands away. 'You will listen to what I have to say and you will listen in silence. If it's the only thing I do for you all this week, it will be to help you realise you're a person in your own right. You said you couldn't be bought and you couldn't be sold. Well, you little fool,' he snapped, shaking her, 'you *have* been bought . . . and sold . . . over and over, by your father and the Webster Corporation.'

'That's a lie, a jealous lie! Why do you insist on pretending that you know so damned much about me? Is it because of the horse,' she sobbed, her control finally snapping, 'or is it because I bought Mr Harrington's property? Why do you hate me so much?' she pleaded, searching for an answer in the fathomless depths of his incredibly dark eyes. A shadow seemed to pass over them, but she failed to understand its meaning before it was lost from her view.

'I don't hate you,' he answered at last, his voice so low she had to lean forward to catch the words. 'Until the programming has been reversed, you'll never be free, you will remain for ever a corporate lady.'

Then Victoria knew that the look she had seen pass over his eyes had been a look of pity!

CHAPTER THREE

DUSK settled over the floodswept terrain as silently as a secret messenger, casting shadows over the landscape that had escaped the floods, so that everything soon became one silent mass of sleeping black velvet.

Inside the little shack Victoria sat hunched in a corner of her cot, legs drawn up to her chin and her small thin arms hugging them against her chest. She watched the approaching dusk with great relief, seeing it reach out to touch and encompass every part of the room until at long last all was enclosed in a protective shroud of darkness.

She began to relax, to settle into the gloom as though she had been born to it like some nocturnal creature, her features soft and pensive, her mind lost in melancholy thought. How could this be happening to her of all people? She thought despondently. Her life had followed a carefully regulated plan, each event almost a non-event, so meticulous was the blueprint of her life. To be thrust into a situation such as she now found herself in was like a ship that had lost its navigator and been left to flounder helplessly in a sea of uncertainty. She was out of her depth with this man who called himself Nicholas Sangster and who seemed determined to force her into areas she had never before wished to explore, or for that matter had even considered challenging. What a crazy stroke of fate that their paths had even crossed! If they had met anywhere else then she was certain he would never had spared her a glance. By the end of the week, when the floods receded and she was free to go, they would never see one another again.

What was his purpose, therefore, in trying to change her thinking, deliberately throwing a wrench into the smooth-running mechanics of her life?

What would she be left with, she wondered, if she began suspecting her father of dealing unethically in business? Would she be doomed to a life of wondering . . . watching . . . waiting? While Nicholas passed his life in this secluded and peaceful setting, she would spend hers in a state of limbo, never really knowing if the seeds of suspicion planted now in her mind were sown there out of malicious intent, desire for revenge, or if they were based on truths. She hugged her knees even closer to her chest. Had her father bought and sold her, had he been using her all these years, conditioning and programming her to think as he thought . . . to destroy, as he destroyed? She shuddered while great spasms of shame rippled through her body. How could she even think such things? It wasn't her father she should be wondering about, it was Nicholas Sangster. Any man who deliberately set out to turn a daughter against her own father must surely be an agent for the devil! And hadn't she read somewhere that the devil *pitied* those who refused to be converted? She felt herself relaxing as though a great burden had been lifted from her shoulders. It was Nicholas Sangster she must guard against, not her father. Better a week with the devil's agent then a lifetime of suffering her father's wrath if ever he should learn she had doubted him even for a moment.

A half smile formed on her lips while a plan began to take shape in her mind. She would show this man Nicholas Sangster what it was like to be cooped up with the daughter of Malcolm Webster! By the end of the week he would have wished he had kept his views to himself, that there was nothing to be gained in provoking a Webster! She didn't know exactly how she would perform this stunt, but she was certain that opportunities would come her way and that Nicholas himself would provide them.

She stretched her legs, easing the cramped muscles while she thought longingly of a hot bath, a shampoo and a change of clothing. These were necessities of life, and as she was in Nicholas' care, it was up to him to furnish her with these basic needs.

They hadn't spoken to each other since late afternoon, but a corner of Victoria's brain had kept track of Nicholas' movements. She knew that he had spoken several times on the CB radio, the rich timbre of his voice drifting across the yard to reach inside the shack. She hadn't tried to follow any of his conversations, not only because none of the words had been audible but because she had been forced into a state of shocked disbelief, a stunned tranquillity that had left her immobile.

Several times Nicholas had come into the room, searched for some article or another and then taken it to a central spot in the breezeway, as though he were gathering things to pack. The door connecting the two rooms had been left open and now a rosy glow, probably from the gas lantern, seeped into her room, filling half of it with an inviting cheerfulness that didn't extend to the part she was sitting in.

He brought some kindling wood and knelt in front of the fireplace, coaxing a few vagrant embers to ignite the sticks. Once the fire had started he added some heavier logs, forcing them into position with a poker. The flames licked up, radiating his face and highlighting the strong line of his jaw, the wide cheekbones and the clean sweep of his intelligent brow. As he knelt forward to add even more logs, the fire crackled and hissed, sending out a spray of burning embers on to the slab of cement leading up to the fireplace. With a pair of tongs he retrieved these, picking each burning coal from the slab and tossing it back into the fire.

A devil likes his fire, Victoria reflected wryly, watching with morbid fascination as he filled a black cast-iron pot with water and placed it on a hook hanging from a steel bar that ran the width of the hearth. She was certain flames had touched his hands, but apparently he hadn't noticed, neither drawing back in sudden alarm, nor wincing with unexpected pain. But then she imagined he was quite used to it, living as he did on the land, with all of its relative hardships.

The warmth of the fire cheered her somewhat and the light it sent out caused the room to take on a cosiness it hadn't had in daylight. She felt her earlier melancholy slip from her shoulders, and free of this burden, her stomach reminded her of other obligations.

'I'm hungry,' she told Nicholas as he stood watching the fire. 'I don't suppose you saved me any of whatever it was you were cooking earlier?'

A log started to roll from the fire, so he tended to that before answering. 'I hadn't intended that you should have any, but if you're too hungry to wait for dinner, there's a bit left in the pot on the stove. Just help yourself.'

'Thank you,' she returned graciously as she slipped from the cot and padded across the room to enter the breezeway. The pot was sitting on the little gas burner as he promised, and when she lifted the lid she stared uncertainly at the gooey mass it contained. She scooped a bit up with her finger and after tasting it, decided it was quite delicious, with a unique nutty flavour she had never before experienced. Grabbing a bowl, she ladled into it as much as she could scrape from the bottom and the sides of the pot, sprinkled sugar on top, then sat at the bench and began eating. She was almost finished when Nicholas joined her in the room. Taking the lid off the pot, he peered inside, then glanced at the empty bowl in front of her. 'You *were* hungry,' he said, as though surprised she had spoken the truth. 'You've licked the pot and the bowl clean as a whistle. Was it good?'

'Delicious,' she smiled. 'You really are a very good cook. I hope you weren't coming back for seconds. I wouldn't have taken it all if I thought you were still hungry,' she apologised. She was feeling generous; the fire, the room with its new-found cosiness and a full tummy all contributing to her state of euphoria. Also she couldn't help but derive a little satisfaction out of knowing she had cheated him out of a second helping.

'Oh, don't worry about it,' he insisted heartily, as she licked the last little drop from her spoon. 'I never eat the stuff myself, but I've heard of others enjoying it.'

'Did you cook it just for me, then?' she asked, as a feeling of unexpected pleasure surged through her being.

'No, actually I never even had you in mind while I was preparing it,' he answered casually, going to the small battery-operated fridge and taking out an oversized pork chop.

'But . . . but . . . if you don't eat it and you didn't cook it for me, who . . . who *did* you cook it for?' she enquired, greatly puzzled.

'The chickens. I prepare them a hot mash every evening during the rainy season. It helps keep them warm and they lay better.'

Her mouth sagged in horror, then she clasped her hands to her neck and gasped. '*Ch-chicken food!?* Oh, my God, I've been poisoned! You *poisoned* me!'

Nicholas pretended to study her carefully, then

announced. 'No, you'll be fine. I only use the finest of ingredients, but tell me truthfully now, I've often wondered . . . is it as good as you say? The chickens seem to like it all right, but you never really know with chickens. Could you suggest something, perhaps? A bit more bran, or maybe the corn kernels could be chopped into finer beak-size pieces?'

Gathering what little composure she had left, she got to her feet and faced him squarely, her large grey eyes betraying her hurt and humiliation, but her voice was steady as she spoke. 'You apparently lack confidence, Nicholas. What can I tell you that the chickens already haven't? Now, if you'll excuse me, I'll take that bath you offered earlier.'

He cut her off at the door, blocking the entry into the other room. Annoyed, she tried to push past him, realising as she did that any actions would be futile, but she was determined to at least try. Then suddenly she stood quite still. What was she doing? she asked herself, engaging in horseplay with this man. If he didn't want her to pass, then she would simply wait until he tired of guarding the door. Folding her arms across her chest and crossing her ankles, she leaned against the door jamb as she had seen him doing, once before. Now all I need do is whistle a catchy little tune, she thought happily, her action and her thought filling her with an unexpected thrill of victory. Her moment of triumph was effectively diluted with Nicholas' casual response, however: 'You shall have your bath, but not yet,' he admonished. 'I think you have a tendency to forget that you're not at home and that luxuries taken for granted there are not so easily available here.'

She smiled. 'I can assure you, Mr Sangster, that it would be quite impossible for me to forget that I'm not at home.'

'Good.' His smile matched hers for coldness. 'Then you'll be patient while the water heating over the fire place comes to a boil? It gets rather chilly at night and I decided you might appreciate bathing in warm rather than cold water.'

'How kind,' she murmured sweetly. 'But where am I to have this bath?' she enquired innocently, looking around. 'I'm certain even your largest bowl wouldn't accommodate me, and even if you found one that did, it would most probably be cracked and chipped like all the others and leak on to the floor.'

'Oh, I've got a very special container for you to bathe in,' Nicholas assured her as he began preparations for his meal. 'Now sit down here like a good girl and keep me company while I have some dinner. I want to keep an eye on you so you don't do anything foolish like trying to lift the pot from the fireplace and scalding yourself.'

She sat on the chair he had indicated and watched while he prepared his meal. From a bottom cupboard he retrieved a box containing various vegetables and from this he selected potatoes, carrots and some fresh beans. He peeled the potatoes and carrots, snipped the ends from the beans, placed them all in a pot, added some water and ignited the fire underneath. Soon the vegetables were bubbling merrily and the aroma from these blended tantalisingly with the sweet-smelling pork chop browning in a black cast-iron frying pan.

With the expertise of a Cordon Bleu chef, he arranged the freshly cooked vegetables onto a plate and then added the chop still sizzling from the pan. From a small earthenware crockpot, he spooned some homemade apple sauce next to the chop, then sat in front of it, knife and fork poised and ready to eat. 'There's no accounting for some people's taste, now is there?' he drawled conversationally after he had swallowed a portion of the succulent-looking chop and started on the fresh vegetables. '*I* like a good thick steak or a tender juicy chop along with a salad or fresh vegetables.'

He continued eating while Victoria desperately avoided looking at his plate to keep herself from drooling. For the life of her she couldn't remember seeing or smelling any meal that looked as good as it most certainly must taste, if Nicholas' obvious enjoyment was any indicator.

'I had planned to be here for at least two weeks,' he continued, but this time his voice was more confiding than conversational, 'so I have plenty of food. But I'm a bit short on laying mash and I might have to restrict your intake, give you smaller portions. I have a sack of oats, though, that I brought along for Dynamite. We could supplement your feed with that. Do you like oats?' he asked seriously, before popping the last of the chop into his mouth.

'So long as I'm alive by the end of the week I really don't care *what* I eat,' she answered with an air of non-chalance she hoped was convincing. 'And as long as I'm not forced to sit and watch your disgusting manners as you stuff yourself, I don't even care *where* I eat,' she added triumphantly.

'I know what you mean,' he agreed soberly. 'Even now while I think of it, I shudder at the memory of you licking that sticky gruel from the spoon. If I hadn't been in the other room, I would have had to watch you go through the whole bowl!'

His eyes glittered across to her, dark with amusement and unshed laughter, while hers stared back devoid of any merriment whatsoever.

'I bet you were a rotten kid,' she grated through clenched teeth as she pushed her stool away from the table. 'If you are quite finished, I'm certain the water must be hot enough for my bath.'

Nicholas reached a long arm across the table and gently grasped her wrist, pulling her towards him. His touch disturbed her causing shivers to race up and down her arm. But it was his eyes that held her attention, paralising her into a state of helpless hypnotic immobility. 'Please sit down, Victoria,' he said softly. 'I'll make your dinner.'

Simple words spoken in a gentle manner can often have the effect of breaking down barriers that no amount of force or other means of persuasion is capable of. Brought up with a lifetime of commands and 'no-nonsense now, you'll do as I say', Victoria was now ripe for love, for kindness, for gentleness. Like a child starved, she had grabbed these commodities from Nicholas when he had offered them, but each time he had snatched them away. Now he was offering them again, only this time she didn't trust him. She was constructing her own barriers now and this time her father had nothing to do with it.

'No, thank you,' she answered simply. 'I'm not hungry, just tired and still a bit sore from my spill off Dynamite, but nothing that a hot bath shouldn't take care of.'

She waited expectantly for some sort of reaction that mention of the horses would bring. When nothing happened she felt unqualified relief, then perversely became angry that the object of so much scorn directed at her should suddenly be of no consequence, and she felt the need to goad him into some sort of provocation. 'I thought you said this was your home, but you mentioned you expected to be here for only two weeks. Does that mean you hop from shack to shack whenever the mood takes you, or does it mean the devil is chasing you?'

Nicholas laughed and let go of her wrist, leaving her free to leave the room, but oddly enough she preferred to stay, content to watch while he cleared the table and washed the dishes. She made no offer to help and he didn't invite her assistance, but she made an attentive audience while he worked and while he worked he explained the situation of the shack and also of Dynamite. 'Dynamite was purchased over six months ago and should have been safely tucked up at the Estate by now, but things sometimes have a way of going wrong. For instance, there was a mix-up at one of the international airports and they 'lost' him for three days. When that mess was finally sorted out, they dropped him off at Sydney instead of Brisbane and he spent much longer than is customary in quarantine, which is a usual procedure for animals purchased outside the country. Anyway, to make a long story short, by the time Dynamite finally made it here, the wet had come and it was impossible to get the trailer and him up the steep hills leading to the property. That's how you happened to come across Dynamite at Harrington's place—Teddy was allowing us to keep him there until we got this place suitably equipped with feed and fences. After all the poor beast had been through, we thought it would be a good idea to bunk him down here for a while and let him rest, get used to the climate and to someone from the Estate.'

'And that's why you're here,' Victoria added conclusively, 'because Dynamite was supposed to be here. So,' she continued, 'this isn't your home after all. You live on an Estate. What are you, then? A horse trainer?'

'I guess you could call me that, but on a homestead you do many things, all of them important—ride fences, clear land, muster cattle. All very different from your way of life, Miss Victoria Webster.'

'Yes, it would certainly be different, but it sounds . . . exciting and healthy. Do you like your job, Nicholas? I mean, it must be hard work repairing fences and training horses and still find time to muster cattle.'

'It keeps me busy,' he admitted with a careless shrug of broad shoulders, 'but as it's the only life I've ever known I don't consider it hard, just challenging.'

'But what do you like doing best?' she asked, suddenly anxious to find out as much as she could about this dark, mysterious stranger. 'I bet it's training horses. Is it?' she asked eagerly.

He smiled down at her, at the expectant almost childish face that peered up at him. 'Yes,' he agreed, 'training horses is one of my favourite pastimes.'

'Pastime?' she echoed. 'But wouldn't it be your life's work, your livelihood?'

'That too,' he admitted, and then, 'Why the sudden interest?'

'Oh, I don't know,' she answered slowly. 'I just thought it would be nice to know something about you, so we would have things to talk about and maybe find a common interest.'

'We already have a common interest,' he pointed out. 'Surely you haven't forgotten that Dynamite is out there somewhere stumbling around in the dark, maybe sick, maybe injured and . . .'

'And that it's my fault,' she broke in with a bitter laugh. 'I haven't forgotten, how could I with you here to constantly remind me? Well, I hope you do find him and that he's in perfect shape,' she lashed out defiantly, 'because I'll grab him and ride out of here!'

Nicholas stared at her for a long, cold moment, his lips an angry tight line in his face. 'If I'm lucky enough to find that horse, Miss Webster, and if I'm able to get him back here I can assure you that if you so much as touch him with one little finger, you will regret it.'

She took a step backward frightened by his menacing words. Surely he must realise that she would never even consider taking the horse, that she had only said what she had to goad him, because it was obvious that he still believed she had taken the horse in the first place, that the horse had not been offered to her.

'No matter what I say or do you refuse to give me the benefit of the doubt—well, I don't care,' she answered heatedly, 'but as far as threatening goes, I wouldn't try it if I were you. Words don't frighten me,' she finished stoutly, drawing herself up to her full height, which didn't quite meet his shoulders.

He looked at her steadily, eyes slightly narrowed. Then a lazy smile tugged at the corners of his mouth, softening the tight line of his lips but doing nothing for the frosty look in his eyes. 'Make no mistake, girl, I wasn't threatening you, I was promising you, and I don't use words to mete out punishment.' He reached out to stroke the soft, sweet curve of her cheek and then lightly passed his fingers over her trembling lips. 'I have something far more effective than that,' he assured her with a smile that left no doubt in her mind as to what that punishment would be.

'You wouldn't dare!' she gasped, her eyes mirroring disbelief.

'Don't tempt me, Victoria, and there'll be no need for dares *or* threats,' he promised, 'but if you insist on provoking me, then I'll be left with no alternative other than to respond in kind.'

'B-But what . . . what would you do?' she whispered, barely able to force the words from her constricted throat, but knowing the question must be asked, for whatever reason she wasn't sure. Perhaps just to be told her suspicions were unfounded.

He smiled that mocking smile that she was growing to detest. 'I would thrash you,' he answered softly, 'long enough and hard enough until you understood that you must not take what doesn't belong to you!'

'Oh, is that all?' she let out in a long relieved sigh. 'I was terrified you meant . . . something else.'

'Did you think I meant to make love to you as a means of punishment?' he asked incredulously. 'My God, Victoria, you're more twisted then I gave you credit for!'

'Twisted? Because I would consider a beating more preferable to your overtures? This may come as a shock to your inflated male ego, but women can strike their own blows, and I think I've just struck one where it hurts most, I've dented that arrogant male pride, haven't I? Fancy any woman not wanting a bohemian like you to . . . to touch her!' she spat sarcastically.

'You can't say it, can you?' he asked wonderingly. 'You really can't get the words out.'

'What words, for goodness' sake? *Now* what are you talking about?' she asked in exasperation.

'Make love . . . making love . . . sex . . . sleeping together . . . those kinds of words.'

Victoria was caught off guard, the bluntness of his accusation filling her with an embarrassment that was only made more unbearable by the close scrutiny of his eyes. He missed not the slightest detail. He saw how her eyes widened with shock, luminous with emotions that he knew to be raging within her. He saw how her cheeks paled and then reddened noticeably and how at last she could no longer meet his eyes, but was forced to look away, while small white teeth chewed cruelly on her bottom lip.

Two long muscular arms snaked out, grabbing her roughly and pressing her against the long hard length of his body. She let out a terrified scream that was quickly and effectively smothered by hard lips that bit into her own. Nicholas' arms crushed her to him, willing her to obey her body responses, but she refused to listen to them, daren't respond to him. His hands began the exploration that had unnerved her before, caressing and coaxing until at last the fires that had been simmering in her since first she met him, blazed with an intensity that almost staggered her. Arms that had hung stiffly by her sides now came slowly, hesitantly up to embrace him, to wrap themselves around his neck, her hands to explore the beautiful shape of his head, fingers to sink into the luxurious thickness of his hair.

His hands moved across her shoulders, down her back and along her thighs, causing flames to shoot through her nerve-stream, and playing havoc with her senses. She moaned and pressed against him, dizzy with the unexpected sensations that her body seemed to crave.

When he finally released her, putting her from him as though she were some unexpected weight that he hadn't expected or wanted to endure, she merely stood there gazing up at him as though bewildered as to where she was.

Neither spoke, content for the moment to gaze at one another, as though to see if the other had understood what had happened. Then, as though from a faraway place, Victoria heard Nicholas' voice. 'The week has barely begun, but I think we can both agree that you're well on your way to becoming a woman.'

Her brain gradually unscrambled itself and his words fell into place as though lodged by a computer, and as clearly as though someone held a message in front of her eyes, she could clearly see the print-out: WRONG. DO NOT BE FOOLED. DO NOT PASS GO. MAN DOES NOT LOVE YOU. USED WRONG CHOICE OF WORDS. SHOULD HAVE SAID 'I LOVE YOU'.

She shook her head, blinking rapidly, and tried desperately to prove the computer wrong. Nicholas did love her, he must do, to hold her and kiss her the way he had. She searched for the unspoken clue in his eyes, the silent message of love . . . but there was nothing, nothing but a smouldering darkness that wasn't love even to her untrained heart, but she did recognise it for what it was. She had seen it before. It was lust, and no other word could explain it. Her heart twisted painfully in her chest, but he must never know what he had done to her.

'I was a woman long before I had the misfortune of entering your life, Nicholas Sangster, and my only hope is that I'll emerge from this shack as pure and as clean as I entered!' She had been tracing a pattern with her toe while she spoke and as she kept her eyes averted from his, head bowed, he could only assume it was because she was shy.

'Come now, Victoria,' he laughed, cupping her chin with his hand and forcing her to look at him. 'If you want to remain in the Victorian age and defend your virtue for ever that's fine with me. I'm certainly not going to rape you, if that's what you think lovemaking is all about. Despite what you've been told or taught, there is a difference, little one.'

She pulled herself away and walked towards the table feeling the need for some distance between them. 'Of course I know there's a difference,' she admitted, without realising she needn't have bothered. Her words only proved to him that his allegations were true. 'It would be foolish of me to pretend that I've had plenty of men, because I haven't, a fact which I'm sure you've already guessed. I . . . I haven't even had one proper boy-friend, would you believe that?' she asked through a shaky little laugh of embarrassment. 'I've been so busy . . . studying and working, that there never seemed time to develop a proper relationship, one that would lead to . . . to . . . lovemaking,' she confessed, cheeks blazing with colour and shock that she had revealed so much about herself. When he didn't answer, she became peeved. 'I suppose you're thinking I blame overwork and studying as a reason for not having had a boy-friend, while really it's because I'm not very attractive, and who would want to get involved with a Webster anyhow? Is that what you're thinking?' she demanded angrily, hands clenched into two tiny fists at her sides.

What was she doing, she thought, confessing like a forlorn, love-starved, middle-aged wench? God, she was only twenty and she was making herself sound like some dumpy twerp who had never had a meaningful relationship!

Meaningful? What did 'meaningful' mean, and why was she torturing herself with these ridiculous thoughts? she wondered in a fit of anguish and despair. Was it possible, really possible, that she *wanted* an affair, and with *him*?

She peeped at him through the corner of one eye. He was so handsome, not in the conventional Hollywood style, but in a rugged, self-assured way that left no doubt as to his potent virility. But how could a man of his obvious good looks escape marriage? He must have women chasing him all the time, only too eager to share his name with him. Or was he married? The thought struck her like a bombshell, knocking the wind from her lungs. Then incredibly she heard herself blurt: 'Are you married?' Now why had she asked him *that*? she groaned inwardly. Things were going from bad to worse. She had sounded like a suspicious girl-friend! 'Never mind,' she waved her question aside, 'I'm being rude and there's no excuse for it, except I'm tired I guess and—well, I wish I had my clothing here with me and . . . and my toothbrush, my brush, my comb and . . . and all my things.'

She wrung her hands in despair as she pleaded with her eyes for him to understand. She really was tired, more tired than she could ever remember being, and all he could do was just to stand there, looking at her as though she had lost all her marbles, or maybe it wasn't that after all. Maybe he really did pity her. Well, let him, she thought miserably. Perhaps his pity will prompt him into getting that bath he's been promising all day.

Then she found herself in his arms again, only this time he was being extremely gentle, carrying her as though she were a baby and walking with her into the small room with the fireplace and laying her softly on to her cot.

'You have every reason for being exhausted, little one. You're distraught, and sleep will expel the day's worries.' He smiled at her, then reached down to stroke the tangled hair away from the perfect oval of her face. Her eyes were large as she gazed helplessly up at him and when he pulled the quilt up and tucked it under her chin, she smiled wistfully.

It was the first time in all her life that she could remember being tucked in. Nicholas watched as she slipped into a peaceful slumber, and she was never to know that he stayed by her side until early morning, until the roosters began to crow and until the sun heralded its blessing on the floodswept terrain of their secluded island.

CHAPTER FOUR

It was well past noon when Victoria finally awoke. She lay on the narrow cot blinking at the unfamiliarity of her monklike surroundings. Sunlight streamed through the irregular shape of the tiny window panes, catching the particles of dust that hovered in the still air.

A sixth sense warned her that she was alone, but still she strained her ears for any sounds that might prove her wrong. But Nicholas wasn't chopping wood, or tending to chores that had kept him busy most of the day before.

All around her there was a stillness that was peaceful rather than foreboding. She threw back the quilt and sprang from the cot with all the exuberance of a young person on her first day at camp.

Outside she kept to the boards that formed the paths surrounding the small shack. The jeep was gone, and she followed its tracks until they disappeared on to grassy slopes away from the house. Shading her eyes, she peered into the distance, a slight frown on her face. Only a small area was safe for travelling before mud and water took over. She sighed, remembering how she had guessed that Nicholas must be planning a journey, judging from his movements around the shack yesterday afternoon.

He would be out looking for the horse. Whether it was a wise decision wasn't her choice to make. She knew that she would do exactly the same thing if something she loved had disappeared. She could only hope that both were safe and that Nicholas would be back by nightfall.

She could cope with the day, but she rather doubted she could do the same with the night.

Taking the trail back to the shack, she planned what she would do. A bath most definitely had first priority and she spent some time before finding something suitable to bathe in. An old round tub made with wooden slabs with steel rings around it seemed perfect. She filled this with water from a tap protruding from the water tank next to the shack and after arming herself with toiletries borrowed from Nicholas's supplies, stripped the white shirt from herself and slipped into the cool water.

It was a tight squeeze, but with her legs pulled up and bent at the knees, she found she could fit quite easily. There were advantages to being small after all, she decided with a happy little grin.

It had seemed a pity to waste the sun, so she was bathing outsides next to the shack. The sun streamed down on her and as she splashed water over her neck and shoulders her skin glistened like a baby seal's. After a few futile attempts to wet her hair, she finally gave in and got out of the tub to fetch a pot. Armed with this she emerged from the shack and slipped gratefully into her little bath once more.

Using the pot as a dipper, she managed to soak her hair and give it a thorough washing, using Nicholas's shampoo. But alas, the water was now too soapy to give it the rinsing it needed, so once again she was forced from the tub to stand in front of the water tank, filling the pot with the clear rainwater and rinsing her long golden hair until it squeaked under her hands.

Squeezing as much water as she could from her hair, she flipped it over one smooth shoulder and proceeded to dry herself, rubbing her skin with a vigour that made her whole body glow. Reaching up, she pulled a pink blossom from one of the frangipanni trees and stuck it behind her ear, then wrapped the pink towel she had used to dry herself around her slender form so that it resembled a sarong.

Swinging back to dispose of her bath water, she came face to face with Nicholas. Startled by his sudden appearance, she had no chance to change the expression from her features, so what he saw was a young girl with an unguarded look of happiness in the large grey eyes. The soft, smooth cheeks glowed with health, the swelling from the sun long since gone. Her lips were parted, pink and full against the sparkling whiteness of straight little teeth.

Her look of pleasure increased measurably at the unexpected surprise of seeing Nicholas home and safe. It was only when she realised that she hadn't heard the jeep making its approach and after looking past him to the spot where it should have been parked did she see that the jeep wasn't there.

His clothes were wet and muddy, his boots tied by the laces and strung over his shoulder added proof that he had walked, and a long way, judging by his appearance. His boots must have acted as undesirable weights; bogging him down in the sticky mud. So he had removed them.

'You've been walking!' she accused, as though it were the most miraculous feat she had ever heard anyone doing.

'For miles,' he answered, pushing back his wide-brimmed hat to wipe the sweat from his brow.

'But why? Has the water gone down sufficiently to make walking a possibility, or did the jeep get bogged?' The questions continued to tumble from her lips. 'Did you catch a glimpse of Dynamite? Is he tied up to the jeep somewhere?' she continued anxiously.

'Hey, slow down!' he laughed. 'Give me half a chance and I'll give you some answers. But first I need a long, cold drink.'

She followed him into the breezeway and after he had satisfied his thirst with three full glasses of cold water from the fridge, he endeavoured to fill her in on the morning's events. 'I left a little after dawn,' he began, 'thinking that I could have a quick meander over some of the high country that can't be touched by the flood-waters. The going was tough and several times I was certain I would have to abandon the jeep.' He paused to pour some water into a basin and after rinsing his face and running water over his head, he continued: 'How-ever, I was always able to free the jeep by jamming boards that I'd brought along, under the wheels. I climbed trees to get a better view through the binoculars to see if I could catch sight of Dynamite.'

'And did you?' she asked, when it appeared he wasn't going to continue.

''Fraid not,' he replied slowly, and then added, 'But I wasn't really expecting to. The horse is smart. My hunch is that he headed up country where it's dry and the feed is plentiful. I have a feeling he's safe.'

'I hope you're right,' she sighed. 'And if it's any consolation, he's terribly strong and certainly isn't lack-ing in spirit. You might have difficulty tracking him down, but I'm sure once he's found he'll be none the worse for wear.'

'Mmm,' he drawled. 'If he stays away from rusty fences or anything that he could cut himself on, then he stands a chance. But in this heat and humidity, one scratch and parasites set in. He could be driven mad!'

Victoria shuddered at the thought, picturing poor Dynamite with millions of flies and mosquitoes feasting on his handsome hide. Nicholas was sitting on a stool facing her, his large brown hands dangling between his knees. He looked exhausted, and her heart reached out to him. Despite everything, it was her fault that Dynamite was lost. The horses in Harrington's stables were little better than mules, and that was why she had admired Dynamite. He was obviously in a class of his own. If only she hadn't hung around the corral where the horse had been enclosed! If only she hadn't accepted his offer of having a ride, if only . . . if only . . . she could go on for ever, but nothing changed the fact that she had taken the horse and that it hadn't been Harrington's to offer and she had let it get away from her, no matter under what circumstances.

And Nicholas had been out searching for him since dawn, he had said, and she knew he would not rest until the horse was found. He would go again and again into the flood-drenched wilderness, risking his own life in the hopes of finding the animal.

'Was . . . was Dynamite insured?' she asked hesitantly, praying that Nicholas wouldn't draw his own conclusions as to why she would ask.

'Yes, of course he was. Why?' he demanded bluntly, but this time she knew he wasn't annoyed with her, just extremely tired.

'I was thinking of your employer and whether or not you would be blamed directly for Dynamite's disappearance. If . . . Dynamite isn't found—but I'm sure he will be,' she hastened to add at the sight of Nicholas' glowering eyes attached to her face, 'then it would make a difference if your employer could recoup his losses. It was just a thought really,' she finished lamely, as Nicholas' eyes grew cold and cruel in his face.

'The basic Webster philosophy,' he answered softly. 'Money takes care of everything, doesn't it?' He ran a hand through his thick black hair. 'You almost had me fooled,' he continued. 'I was beginning to think that perhaps I'd misjudged you, that you were just a poor misguided kid that hadn't really had a fair chance to grow to be her own person. But I see I was wrong. You *are* a Webster after all. Money is the healer, the anecdote against all pain. Well, Miss Webster, money can't buy a dream, nor can it take the place of a dream that's been lost!'

'No,' she agreed coolly, 'but it can replace it with another!' Her heart wrenched at the look of disgust on his face. She walked over to the screened-in section of the room standing with her back towards him, looking towards the old fiddlewood tree. 'Do you remember yesterday when you were showing me around the property?' she asked softly. 'We were under that old fiddlewood tree out there and I told you about the wonderfully happy feeling I was having. You told me that you had the same feeling when you were on your way to pick up Dynamite. My happy feeling disappeared . . . because I knew you weren't happy.'

She was silent for a while and then she spoke again. 'I've had dreams,' she confessed, 'wonderful dreams. When I was very young I used to dream that my mother wasn't dead, that she would come back to me with all sorts of wonderful surprises. I used to dream that one day I would be allowed to attend school with other kids instead of having private tutors. I used to dream that my whole life was a dream and that I would wake up one morning to find myself with brothers and sisters and two parents all sitting around a cosy little kitchen table. My mother would turn to me and say I looked flushed or something like that and insist I stay home from school. Then we'd bake a cake and I would lick the spoon.' She laughed softly. 'Do you want to know where I got that dream from?' she asked, turning towards him. 'From a television commercial! So you see, Nicholas, no one knows better than I that money can't buy a dream, at least not the kinds of dreams I grew up longing for. But your dream is *insured*, Nicholas. You're very lucky, you know. Most dreams aren't!'

'You amaze me, you really do,' he answered with an appreciative smile. 'For someone as small as you and still so young, you really know how to play your cards.'

Confused, Victoria could only stammer, 'Wh-what do you mean by that?'

He laughed again, getting to his feet and going over to her. Placing two lean-fingered hands on her shoulders, he lowered his head so that black eyes challenged grey. She trembled at his touch, at his body so close to her own treacherous one. Swallowing hard, she willed herself not to give anything away, not even the slightest hint of how his merest touch affected her.

'You almost blew it, didn't you?' he chuckled mockingly. 'Your suggestion that perhaps Dynamite might bring more in real terms let the cat out of the bag. Is that another trick under the heading of Webster Ethics?' he sneered. 'Buy, insure, lose and collect at a healthy profit?'

'Why, you despicable . . . I've never known a nastier person!' she grated, and then, 'I take that back. You're not a person—people like you give all humanity a bad name. You're a dirty, filthy, lying *beast*, and although I've never hated anyone, I do now, and I *like* the feeling!'

With that, she attempted to twist from his grasp, but he wasn't finished with her yet. 'While we're handing out compliments, Miss Webster, I have one for you. Your little scenario was very touching, but it lacked conviction. Somehow, the "poor little rich girl" act just doesn't fit.'

She brought her hand up and would have landed a
healthy blow had he not anticipated her action. 'I've
been waiting for you to try something like that,' he
smiled coldly, catching her wrist in his hand. She paled
as his fingers bit cruelly into the fragile bones of her arm,
but she said nothing, unwilling to give him the satisfaction of knowing he was hurting her. Then he brought her
hand up to his lips and gently kissed each of her fingertips. 'Isn't there something else you wanted to ask me,
Victoria?' he asked.

Her brows knitted together in a puzzled frown, but
she said nothing. She could feel his breath against her
hand, and although she hated herself for it, she wanted
him to go on kissing her fingers. What strange power did
this man hold over her? She wondered, as she shook her
head helplessly while again Nicholas repeated his question, following with,

'You haven't asked me about the jeep,' he reminded
her. 'It's lying under at least fifteen feet of mud. It was
old,' he shrugged, 'but it was insured. Do you think I'll
collect enough to buy a new one?'

Victoria wanted to spit in his cruelly mocking eyes,
but she couldn't bring herself to do it. Instead she
replied:

'Oh, I wouldn't know about jeeps, especially old ones,
but I've heard tell that men carry hefty insurance policies
on *their* lives. And unlike jeeps, they needn't be buried
fifteen feet for someone to collect.'

Nicholas' short, sharp bark of laughter told her he
wasn't amused. 'If you're hinting that my days are
numbered, then I'd better proceed with your lessons.
For instance,' he asked, still holding her wrist and
pulling her into the adjoining room, 'how long do you
intend leaving your clothing to soak before you get
around to washing them?'

She looked gloomily down at the basin holding her clothes that he had removed from her the day before. The water was murky, black with oily rings. She poked a finger into it, pulling out her shirt that was once sparkling white. It was ruined, but she wasn't worried about that.

'H-How did the jeep get buried?' she stammered, not daring to look at him, keeping her eyes on the water in the basin.

She could feel his eyes on her, but still she refused to look up. She was feeling the shock of learning about the jeep and the realisation of the danger he must have been in. But if she had offered sympathy, she knew he would only have sneered at her words.

'There was a landslide,' he explained casually, as though landslides like traffic jams were every day occurrences. 'We're safe where we are, but weeks of steady rain has corroded the banks of some of the smaller hills, causing them to topple like children's sand castles.'

'You might have been killed!' she exclaimed with a shudder.

'And that distresses you, does it?' he asked mockingly. 'Why I wonder? Could it be that the idea of being here on your own fills you with dread? No one to fetch and carry for the spoilt daughter of Malcolm Webster?'

Victoria sighed and twirled the lightweight slacks around the basin. They were no longer the pale yellow they had started out to be. 'Of course,' she murmured, 'what other reason could there be?'

'None that I can think of,' he replied casually tilting her chin with the crook of a finger to look into her eyes and then at the soft pink mouth that was trembling slightly, 'unless, of course, you're beginning to realise you were never intended to lead the life of a corporation zombie, that inside that frozen exterior you've been trained to present, there's a woman who's bursting to be set free, who's had a taste of what it feels like to have blood, instead of ice, coursing through her veins and who wants to be driven to the heights of passion that every woman longs for!'

'Why must you say things like that?' she demanded, flushing. 'You narrowly avoided being buried by a landslide, an event that would horrify anyone on hearing such news. Why must you misconstrue my concern as meaning simply that I would miss having a . . . a man around to . . . to help me cope with nature?'

Nicholas threw his head back and roared with laughter, while Victoria stood watching him, colour rushing to her cheeks. When his unbridled merriment had finally exhausted itself, she said quietly, 'You really do hate me.'

It was a statement spoken in the flat tones used when one comes face to face with the truth. She gazed up at him a look of wonder in the large grey eyes, as though up till now she hadn't really believed that his dislike of her had been so absolute.

'You could be right,' he agreed casually, lifting the basin containing her clothing and walking through with it into the breezeway. Sliding the screen door aside with one hand, he stood in the opening while he dished her clothes out of the filthy water and tossed them into her bath water still resting under the sun. 'But then hate is so close to love, only a fine line dividing the two, that perhaps you should be wondering whether it's love and not hate that prompts me to question you about *your* feelings,' he said softly, catching and holding her eyes across the expanse of the two rooms.

'I think I've already made my feelings regarding you quite clear,' she answered directly. 'The difference between hate and love is easily defined in my mind, if not in yours.'

'Only a person who has experienced neither would admit so freely to understanding both. But then I tend to underestimate the Websters. It's only fitting that you should have the answers that have evaded poets and philosophers for centuries!'

Victoria returned his mocking smile. 'Ah, but poets and philosophers detest simplicity, as you so obviously do. But I find it refreshing, therefore I experience no confusion in separating both and understanding each. In other words Mr Sangster, I *know* what I hate and I *know* what I love.'

'If only that were true, little one, then you would have no need to look so tragic.'

'Oh, for goodness' sake!' she exclaimed, stomping towards him. 'If I appear tragic it's only because I can't believe what's happening here. I woke up this morning to find you gone with not even so much as a note telling me where. Then you appear out of the blue, covered in mud, and calmly explain that the jeep is buried under a landslide. When I voiced concern over your safety, based on the logical conclusion that you might have been killed considering the circumstances—what do you say? You insinuate that I would miss having a . . . a man around to do all the *dirty* work, and I mean that quite literally!'

She was only inches away from him. Wide-eyed, she stared up at him, searching for clues that might prove her words had struck home, had penetrated that thick, unyielding hide. But his features had lost their slightly mocking attitude and now he looked as though he had been carved from stone. His whole body had gone rigid, eyes glittering like cold pieces of steel, and his mouth a hard straight line in his face.

She took a step backwards, suddenly afraid that he might strike her. Her words had had an effect all right, but obviously not in the way she had hoped. She had meant to ridicule him, make him eat humble pie, force him into realising how unfair he was being. She hadn't meant to unleash the devil that had been lurking under a cloak of mild-mannered impudence.

She braced herself, ready to receive any punishment that he might dish out. She held her head high, small chin thrust defiantly upwards, the thick veil of lashes almost obscuring the clear grey of her eyes.

Like sparring partners they faced one another, and then Nicholas' features relaxed. A long, ragged sigh escaped from his throat as though he had been holding his breath for a very long time. His eyes lost their coldness, a kindly, tolerant look replacing the steely hardness. His mouth relaxed into a smile.

'Despite all proof to the contrary, I fooled myself into believing you were a woman with normal needs. I believed that before the week was over I would have you in my bed, that we would make love because we both wanted to, but I know now I was wrong.' He ran a hand through the thick scrub of his hair and Victoria saw, as though watching from a dream, that his hand was trembling. 'You're safe, Victoria, so you may as well relax. No man wants to tangle with a woman who regards sex as something dirty and sordid and to be avoided at all cost.'

Her jaw dropped open and then snapped shut. She shook her head helplessly as words formed in her brain, but refused to come from her mouth. As though sensing her plight, but not the reason why, Nicholas reached out and lightly stroked her cheek, and tucking a few wisps of hair behind her ear. His hand strayed to the back of her head, down the slender column of her neck, across the silky smoothness of her back to finally rest on one

rounded shoulder. Her heart lurched at his smile, at the
nearness of his mouth so close to her own. His caressing
hand had stirred her senses to give lie to his words, but
he wasn't to know this. 'You're trembling,' he acknowledged, a wicked gleam in his eyes. His hand reached up
to touch the throbbing pulse at the base of her throat and
he nodded as though in answer to a question that only he
had a right to understand.

'You're lovely, Victoria,' he breathed, his hand moving to encircle the nape of her head. 'Much too lovely to
waste, to be old before your time, shackled to your
father and the Webster Corporation.'

She knew she should move away, but her body had
become immune to her brain's commands. It was as
though his touch held a mysterious power over her, a
touch so potent that she was rendered spineless, a
quivering bowl of jelly.

His hand moved from her head to slide once more
down her neck to cup her face in his hand. Helplessly,
she gazed into the black coals of his eyes, her own eyes
glazed with the storms of passion that she was trying so
desperately to deny. Her lips parted in an unconscious
gesture to receive the kiss that must surely come. Her
eyes closed as she sagged towards him. She felt the
warmth of his breath against her ear and then his mouth
moved across her cheek to rest teasingly against her lips.

Then, to her horror, she heard him laugh. A low,
sinister chuckle coming from deep within his throat. Her
eyes flew open, startled and bewildered by his callous-
ness, while a deep-rooted sense of shame swept throughout her body at the sight of the undisguised triumph in
his eyes. 'You are a rosebud,' he said, not giving her a
chance to regain her composure. 'A little pink rosebud
who needs to blossom, but hides her face from the sun!'

Victoria broke easily from his hold and Nicholas made

no attempt to stop her as she ran blindly from the room to seek refuge against those tauntingly cruel eyes and the deep rumbling of amused laughter.

So, it was all a game, she thought disparagingly, pressing white knuckles against the red-hot flames of her cheeks. Her eyes were unnaturally bright as she relived the horrible scene of yielding to him, practically begging for his kiss, while all along he was laughing at her. His caresses that had sent shivers racing throughout her body had only been a ploy to prove to *himself* that she wanted him. He had deliberately set her up, without any regard to her feelings, so he could prove a point. He was ruthless, evil, a predator with no respect for humanity.

How could she go back into that shack with both of them knowing what he had done and the reason why? It would be like living with a monster, never knowing when it would reveal its ugly head. Whenever he looked at her, he would remember how she practically threw herself at him and whenever he smiled or laughed, she would think he was laughing at her.

She groaned and hid her burning face in her hands, imagining how he would enjoy her attempts to avoid him, to step out of his way whenever he came close, to always be looking the other way whenever she chanced to glance in his direction.

'Damn you, Dynamite, and damn you, Teddy Harrington, for getting me into this mess!' she moaned aloud, cradling her aching head in her arms as she folded them around her knees.

'Regrets, Miss Webster?' came a coldly sardonic voice above her head. 'Surely you don't blame a horse and a man for your own misguided emotions? Especially,' Nicholas continued smoothly in a voice that led her to believe he would enjoy seeing her squirm, 'a horse now in grave danger because you had a few idle moments to fill in between ripping off Harrington and waiting for a lift to the airport!'

His words, she decided, weren't worthy of comment, so she jumped to her feet intending to race towards the shack. But his arm snaked out to grab her wrist and once again she was his prisoner. 'I'm going to have a shower,' he told her casually as he marched her towards the shack, 'and when I'm finished I want to see your clothes washed, rinsed and hanging up to dry.'

Depositing her like some wilful, disobedient child by the bucket containing her clothing, he sauntered off towards the side of the shack, whistling merrily. She watched him go, eyes riveted on the strong, muscular back that was deeply tanned, thinking she could cheerfully strangle him with the towel he had draped carelessly around his neck!

As she bent over the wash bucket to fish her clothing from the water, Victoria wondered if she would ever get over the humiliation she had suffered at the hands of Nicholas Sangster. It hadn't been enough for him, forcing her to behave like a common trollop. Oh no! He had to drag her across the yard as though she were some sort of peasant trying to escape the drudgeries of washday!

Her clothing was ruined, the slacks ripped and her shirt had one pocket missing with the other barely hanging on by a thread. Scooping them into a bundle, she looked around the yard until she saw what she was searching for. With a furtive glance in the direction Nicholas had disappeared, she scampered across the yard and lifting the lid off the garbage bin, dumped her clothes inside. Feeling enormously pleased with her small gesture of defiance, she returned to the small stoop by the wash bucket and picking up the large brown brush owned by her 'master', calmly bent her head forward and began brushing the long golden tresses.

Presently two big feet appeared into her line of vision. Raising her eyes, she saw that the bare feet grew into two brown columns of sturdy muscular legs. Still further up, she blushed with embarrassment at the sight of Nicholas clad only in a towel wrapped around his middle. The black, silky hairs on his chest were still damp, as was the hair falling over his forehead, giving him a curiously boyish look.

His grin caught her unawares, the strong white teeth flashing against the healthy tan of his skin. He seemed relaxed, totally at ease with his world, and as he bent forward to grab a handful of her hair, his grin changed into a smile as he watched the silky strands sift through his fingers. 'You're beautiful and your hair is beautiful. You are, without doubt, the most beautiful little rosebud I've ever seen.'

God forgive her, Victoria thought, as she found herself blushing with pleasure and returning, actually returning, his smile. God, she had never realised she was so *weak*!

'Thanks,' she heard herself murmuring. 'My mother had this colour hair, but apparently hers was much thicker. I—I used to worry that mine was too fine, but I guess it's not, although it won't hold a curl. Th-that's why I wear it this way, straight and long, although I don't believe it's quite the fashion,' she finished on a limp note.

Biting her tongue to keep herself from further inane babblings, she bowed her head to watch while her toe traced little patterns in the dirt. Was that really herself, she thought disgustedly, talking about her hair as though she were a teenager receiving her first compliment.

Of course it wasn't *her,* she rallied to her defence. It was Nicholas' fault, the strange hold he had on her, that was responsible for her irrational behaviour. Never before had she ever behaved so giddily stupidly, blushing and stammering at every turn. Perhaps by the end of the week she would have more of a hold on herself and Nicholas could see for himself that she was a sane, normal, intelligent young woman, and then maybe, just maybe, he might have the grace to apologise for his barbarism and uncompromising manner towards her.

'I see you haven't done your washing,' he was saying, and she followed his eyes to the empty stretch of line that hung precariously between two saplings. Then both their eyes returned to the bucket and Victoria suppressed a smile as he bent to swish his hand through the suds.

Her eyes widened in horror, however, as he held out two tiny and barely recognisable undergarments. As she lunged towards him with the intent to grab them from his hands, he merely laughed, holding them out of her reach.

Stretching her bikini panties between two thumbs and holding her bra in the crook of his little finger, he studied them, a bemused expression on his face. 'Now what could these be?' he drawled in his lazy fashion. 'Surely your slacks haven't shrunk,' he queried as he snapped the elastic band of her panties. 'And this,' he asked, holding out her bra, 'could this *really* be what's left of your shirt?'

'Give them to me!' she demanded, feeling the heat burn in her cheeks. But he ignored her, holding the garments high over his head, therefore well out of her reach as he gazed up at them, shaking his head in fascinated wonder.

'You know damned well what they are!' she accused him hotly. 'I'll bet you've seen thousands of ladies under-garments, so why the big act?' To embarrass her of course, what other reason would there be. Horrid brute, she thought as a wave of red-hot fury gripped her.

'Ladies undergarments?' he queried, fixing her with wide, innocent eyes. 'But they're so *small* how could a *lady* wear something so,' he pursed his lips as he thought, 'so scanty!'

Victoria blushed to the tips of her pink little ears. 'They are *not* scanty! What do you expect me to wear in this heat? Bloomers?' she snapped.

Nicholas shuddered. 'Definitely not bloomers,' he snorted. 'With your skinny little legs you'd look like Minnie Mouse.' He looked down at her. 'But of course I recognise them now,' he admitted, his eyes bright with mischievous laughter. 'You were wearing them when I undressed you. I'm afraid I didn't pay much attention because I was more concerned with any injuries your sweet little body might have sustained.'

'I'll just bet!' she rasped through clenched teeth. 'It positively makes me sick to think of you *leering* at me while I wasn't in a position to do anything about it.'

He nodded. 'I can understand that,' he said, goading her. 'I considered blindfolding myself, but then I wouldn't have known where to place my hands. You see, I was checking for cracked ribs, that sort of thing.'

She glared at him while he walked over to the water tank and rinsed the brief garments under the tap and then pegged them to the line. They fluttered in the soft breeze like two little banners heralding their new-found freedom.

'Well,' he said rubbing his hands together, 'that takes care of half your wash. Now I wonder where the rest could be?' turning a quizzical brow in her direction.

'I wouldn't know,' she answered frostily, detesting the smug look on his face.

'You're sure?' He rubbed his chin. 'They were in the bucket not more than twenty minutes ago.'

'Beats me,' she shrugged, beginning to enjoy herself.

'You wouldn't have thrown them in the garbage bin, now would you?'

'Now why would I do a thing like that?' she asked sweetly.

'Shall I have a look?' he asked brightly, as though the idea had just occurred to him.

She shifted uneasily on the step. He *knows*, she thought. Heavens, he must have eyes in the back of his head! 'If sifting through rubbish bins is your thing,' she answered in a feeble attempt to dissuade him, 'then by all means, go ahead.'

'Would you like to come?' he offered, extending his hand. 'We could look together.'

'Kind,' she murmured. 'But I'll pass this one up. You go ahead, though,' she urged. 'I'll watch the excitement from here!'

'But it would be so much more fun if you came,' he said, pulling her to her feet and slipping an arm around her shoulder as he led her across the yard to where the bin was standing. 'Shall we have a bet?' he asked. 'The loser gets to wash all the dirty laundry. Yours and mine!'

Visions of the muddy gear he had worn back to the shack swam before her eyes. But he couldn't really force her to wash those, now could he?

'Why not?' she shrugged.

With a flourish Nicholas raised the lid, and at the sight of her bedraggled clothing lying at the bottom of the bin, Victoria raised her hand to her mouth to suppress her laughter. With a long, wooden stick Nicholas fished the garments from the bin and dropped them at her feet.

'Well, well, well,' he drawled, 'they were in the garbage bin, after all.'

'Surprise! Surprise!' she giggled, her shoulders shaking helplessly.

'Pick them up,' he ordered. 'I fail to understand how

you could so carelessly discard your only garments. As appealing as you look in that towel, it's hardly suitable gear in our particular circumstance.'

'Haven't you *any* sense of humour?' she gasped, wiping the tears of laughter from her eyes. 'I was only playing a game, I was going to get them later.'

'Were you? I wonder,' he growled. 'At any rate, if it was some kind of weird joke I'm afraid it backfired. You've given yourself a lot of extra work. Remember our little bet,' he flung over his shoulder as he sauntered back towards the shack.

'Spoilsport!' muttered Victoria, sticking her tongue out at his retreating figure, before stooping to pick up her clothing.

CHAPTER FIVE

ONE hour later, Victoria was still bent over the laundry bucket. Her own clothing done and hanging on the line, she was now working on Nicholas'. She had never realised how uncompromising denim could be. Her knuckles were raw from trying to scrub the mud from them.

Nicholas had appeared at various intervals, offering suggestions, encouragement, and twice he had emptied the blackened water to replace it with new. Now he was calling from the window to tell her lunch would be ready in twenty minutes, and perhaps if she used the scrub brush he had given her, she would be finished in time to eat.

Wiping the perspiration from her brow, she looked up and smiled weakly. Not for the life of her was she going to let on that she was exhausted. She would drop in the bucket and drown before she gave him the satisfaction of seeing her droop!

While she was hanging his clothes on the line, Nicholas came out with a cane basket to gather fruit.

'Fruit salad for dessert,' he said. 'We have paw-paw, bananas, oranges, and there are still a few mangoes left—good Queensland fruit. I hope you're not allergic to any of it, because fruit will have to be our main dessert while we're here.'

'Oh, I love fresh fruit,' she admitted, 'and I can't imagine a nicer dessert.'

She was rinsing her face and splashing water on her arms and the back of her neck, when Nicholas returned with his basket laden with fruit. 'Go easy on that water,' he warned. 'Once these tanks are empty, we have to wait for more rain to fill them, and I hope that won't be for a while yet.'

Guiltily, Victoria turned off the tap and looking sheepish explained: 'I felt so hot—I was just trying to cool off.'

'When you want to wash, let me know and I'll fill a basin for you. Allowing the water to run like that is only wasting it. I saw you did the same thing when you were taking a bath. You left the tap running while you were inside getting a pot and again while you were sitting in the tub.'

Her cheeks blazed with colour. 'You mean . . . you mean you *saw* me taking my bath?'

'From start to finish,' he drawled, a wicked gleam in his eye.

'But that's disgusting!' she flared. 'At least a lady can expect to have a bath without somebody spying on her!'

'True,' he admitted with a nod, while his eyes roamed freely along the slender lines of her body, 'but when a lady decides to bathe outdoors, I think she must expect a certain amount of spying.'

'So you admit it, then,' she rasped. 'You were actually spying on me. Oh, how could you?' she demanded, tears of outrageous indignation springing to her eyes. It seemed more than she could bear to think something as private as a bath had been watched by another.

'You're overreacting, Victoria,' he said, tilting her chin and seeing the treacherous tears sparkling on her lashes. 'You're forgetting I've already seen you stripped, but not in the same happy atmosphere as your obvious enjoyment of your bath, even though you did manage to waste gallons of water.'

His fingers on her chin and the steady gaze of his eyes

on hers caused her heartbeats to quicken, and suddenly she was quite breathless. 'I—I'm sorry about the water,' she managed, as though the water was the prime factor of their discussion and not the fact he had seen her bathe. 'I never thought, I mean I thought you would be away for quite some time, so that's why I was having my bath outside. Besides, the sun was so warm . . . and I guess you weren't really spying, I mean it wasn't your fault I was in your line of vision when you returned,' she finished breathlessly, completely unnerved by his nearness and feeling she would drown in the smouldering hot pools of his eyes.

Later, sitting at her place at the table which had been neatly set and watching while Nicholas chopped up the fruit and put the finishing touches to their meal, she couldn't help but chastise herself for failing so miserably to bring Nicholas to heel. It didn't seem fair that no matter what the issue, she was always the one left to apologise.

His ability to outmanoeuvre her at every turn was discomfiting to say the least, and it didn't help matters any to see him looking so cool and composed dressed casually but neatly in a blue striped T-shirt and navy shorts. By comparison, she felt grubby and untidy wrapped still in the pink towel that looked as though it had come through the same wash as Nicholas' clothing!

The meal was delicious, another point in his favour, Victoria was reluctant to admit. After two helpings of lamb stew and feather-light dumplings, she barely had room to dispose of the large soup bowl filled with the sweet tropical fruits.

'Gosh, that was good,' she admitted wholeheartedly, pushing the bowl away from her. 'If ever you get tired of horse training, you could always open a restaurant!'

He grinned. 'Simple fare served simply is the secret of

my success. Now, if you'll excuse me,' he said, getting to his feet, 'I'm going to work on a map to plan the best routes for tracking down Dynamite.'

'I think I'll take a nap,' she said, stifling a yawn. 'I'm not used to such a large meal in the middle of the day and it's made me sleepy.'

'Fine, but make sure you do the dishes first.'

She blinked. 'The dishes? Why should *I* have to do the dishes?'

'Because *I* made the meal. You're not forgetting that we established right from the beginning that you're not a guest and that we would share equally with the chores?'

'Oh, all right,' she grumbled. 'I've had my hands in water most of the morning, so why not the afternoon as well?'

'I'll fill the dishpan for you,' Nicholas volunteered generously.

'Gee, thanks,' Victoria bit out sarcastically. 'I hope you don't use the same soap for the dishes as you made me use for the laundry,' she said, holding out two red little hands. 'I won't have any skin left at this rate,' she mourned unhappily, turning to survey the mess on the table.

She was just as inexperienced with the mysteries of cleaning up after a meal as she had been with the laundry, so the simple chores of clearing away, sweeping and stacking plates consumed the better part of an hour. By the time the dishes were actually ready to be washed, she decided she had more than done her share.

'Nicholas?' she called out to where he was sitting in the other room, sketching trails on a map.

'Yes?' he answered back.

'The dishes are ready to be washed,' she sang sweetly.

'Congratulations!' he applauded. 'It's taken you an

hour to get them to that state, perhaps it won't take you as long to actually wash them.'

'But I don't think I should have to wash them,' she pouted, standing in the doorway where she could see him.

'Why not?' he asked, making no attempt to mask his annoyance at being interrupted.

'Because you said we were to share the chores equally. I've cleared the table, swept the floor and stacked the dishes. Surely that represents half?'

'Ah, but I *set* the table,' was his quick rejoinder.

'Oh, all right, I'll do them,' she snapped, 'but you'll do them tonight, because I intend to make dinner!'

'Well, if it takes as long for you to prepare a meal as it seems to take for any other job you perform, I suggest you start on it right away if we're to eat before midnight.'

'How can I start on it right away if I've got the darn dishes to do?' she grated, as he bent his head over the maps sprawled in front of him. 'It seems I'm the only one doing all the work around here,' she mumbled, turning back to the dishes.

Finally, with the dishes safely out of the way, Victoria stretched out on her cot with a few of the old magazines from which she intended to find a recipe for their dinner. Nicholas was working at the bench not far from her.

'How does this sound?' she asked, reading a recipe out to him.

He shuffled his papers impatiently. 'A bit too ambitious for you, I would say,' he answered disagreeably.

How dared he insinuate that she couldn't cook! 'Simple fare served simply might be the height of your culinary delights,' she replied heatedly, 'but I'm not so easily satisfied. I like to have my tastebuds teased occasionally.'

'I don't think your tastebuds are the only things you like having teased,' he drawled, 'but at least your admission is a start in the right direction.' His eyes gleamed wickedly across at her and she coloured at his blatantly suggestive remark.

'If you're going to be crude, then I shall remove myself from this room,' she sniffed indignantly, gathering her magazines and making a hasty retreat from the room, while his laughter serenaded her departure.

From the breezeway, she could see her slacks and shirt blowing in the breeze and decided that even if they were still wet, she would feel less vulnerable if she was wearing something familiar and more practical than what she now had on. Besides, she didn't like her undergarments on public display, even though Nicholas was the only member of the public who was likely to see them!

Grabbing her things from the line, she followed the same path she had seen Nicholas take for his shower. Against one side of the shack was a sort of stall equipped with a spray nozzle attached to a hose which hung from a box overhead. Very ingenious, she thought, admiring the crude but adequate contraption. There was even a shower curtain.

Stepping into the stall, she dragged the curtain shut and proceeded to dress, confident that this time she was enjoying total privacy.

After hanging her towel on the line (she would wash it later, maybe tomorrow) she stepped back into the breezeway, feeling more assured than she had since her arrival. She hated to admit that she was grateful to Nicholas for making her retrieve her clothing from the rubbish bin.

Nicholas was standing by the small fridge, two tall glasses of fruit juice in his hands. 'Well,' he remarked, his eyes roaming appraisingly over her figure, 'I see you decided to get dressed.'

'Yes,' she agreed somewhat shyly, his close scrutiny making her feel oddly selfconscious. 'They don't look half bad, do they, considering what they've been through?' she asked, looking down at her shirt and slacks.

'Or where they've *been*!' he reminded her drily as he passed her a glass of the cool-looking liquid.

'Yes—well, let's forget about that little act of folly, shall we?' she asked with a flippant shrug of one dainty little shoulder. 'After all,' she reminded him sardonically, 'I haven't once mentioned *your* little act of folly.'

'Which is?' he asked, leaning against the bench and regarding her with an air of amused mockery.

'Why, losing the jeep, of course! Throwing my clothes in the rubbish bin can hardly compare with *that*!'

She enjoyed watching the dark stain that spread across his cheeks and she made no attempt to hide the gleeful smile that danced playfully along her lips.

'Trust you to compare a wilful act of spoilt disobedience with a mishap that was unavoidable and which could have far-reaching consequences,' he remarked drily.

'Now I see,' she countered evenly, the fine, straight lines of her brows drawn together in a show of perplexity. 'When I do something wrong, it's because I'm spoilt and disobedient, while when you do something, it's an unavoidable mishap, with far-reaching consequences. I can't say I'm surprised, though,' she added carelessly, turning her attention once more to the magazines, before tossing over her shoulder, 'it reeks of the same patronising arrogance I've learned to expect from you.'

'You don't feel that *the accident* involving the jeep should cause us any alarm, then?' Nicholas bit out sarcastically. 'We should treat the whole thing as a lighthearted joke and pretend it doesn't really matter that we're now without transport or any means of communication?'

'Of course I don't mean that!' she lashed out, paling a little at the significance of his words. 'It's just that I feel it was most light*hearted*, if not light*headed*, of you to take the jeep out in the first place. I mean,' she peeped sideways at him, 'you know so much about so many things, myself and the Webster Corporation included, that I find it rather surprising you wouldn't know that mud-slides are likely to occur during the rainy season!'

She glanced smugly across at him, savouring the effect her witty little barbs of sarcasm was having on him. His eyes had narrowed noticeably, she saw, and his mouth was an angry white line in his face. Boldly, she pressed on, eager to balance the scales for all the hurtful accusations he had forced her to endure . . . not to mention her stint at the laundry bucket, or the little matter of the dishes, or the fact that he had spied on her while she was having her bath, and that he had done nothing at all to prevent her eating the chicken mash. It certainly was a good thing for him, she decided generously, that she wasn't your everyday, common type of person, who enjoyed revenge. 'But perhaps I'm being unfair,' she cooed sweetly, flashing a benevolent smile. 'If you were as clever as you apparently think you are, and if I was as dumb as you apparently think I am, then it would be you who had all the wealth that you scorn me for having and I would be the one living in such humble squalor without benefit of labour-saving devices, or electricity, or hot and cold running water. It sure makes you think, doesn't it?' she asked, her face a mask of innocent wonder.

But the small flame of anger she had managed to ignite in him was now gone, she realised reluctantly, as he cast her words aside with as little irritability as if a small fly had suddenly landed on his arm. 'Oh, I would never call the Websters dumb,' he corrected her, 'just devious! Some people find it pleasurable getting rich at the expense of others. The only dollar they love is the one they get that another has broken his back to earn. And as for me thinking that I'm clever,' he added casually, smiling at her, 'only a fool admits to that, or worries what someone else thinks of him. And the only thing that worries me right now is whether or not you intend to make a start on that dinner you've promised.'

'I'm surprised you'd trust me sufficiently to cook for you,' Victoria parried, hurt by his stinging remarks. 'Aren't you terrified that I might poison you?'

'Oh, I don't think a Webster would stoop to *murder!*' he exclaimed with mock horror. 'You prey off the living, not the dead.'

'Just for that, I *won't* cook,' she said crossly, folding her arms across her chest in a stubborn gesture of defiance.

'Yes, you will,' he corrected her, a warning smile on his lips. 'It's obvious you've never washed clothes before, or cleared a table, or washed dishes. I'm willing to bet you've never prepared a meal, either. And the only way I'm going to find *that* out is to have you cook dinner.'

'Well, I lost the other bet, but I won't lose this one,' she answered coyly. 'If I turn out a truly superb meal, then you'll have to do all the cooking *and* the washing up for the rest of the time we're here. How's that?' she gloated triumphantly.

'Sounds great,' he agreed readily, 'but you realise, of course, that if you *don't* turn out a truly superb meal, as you say, then it will be you doing all the cooking and the washing up.'

'I can assure you, *kind* sir, that I don't intend losing

this bet, so I have no worries on that score. Now, if you'll just get out of here, please, the chef will begin.'

Nicholas chuckled. 'To prove I'm not a hard task-master,' he said, heading for the door, 'I won't expect anything too spectacular. Scrambled eggs will do just fine.'

Scrambled eggs, indeed! Victoria fumed inwardly, as frantically she searched through the magazines for a suitable recipe. Finally she found just what she was looking for . . . a three-course dinner for two, with step-by-step instructions for each of the three courses. How could she go wrong?

Happily she stepped out on her first cooking adven-ture. Two hours later she emerged from the breezeway looking as though she had been the major ingredient that had been stewed, steamed, baked and fried!

'Ah, Nicholas,' she said as she pretended to casually wipe her hands on the big, floppy apron that covered her from head to toe, 'those eggs you said you wanted. Scrambled, wasn't it?'

He looked up from the book he was reading, the maps he had been working on, now folded neatly by his arm. Slowly he rose to his feet, the book lying forgotten on the table, as he stared at her in astonishment. 'Good grief!' he ejaculated, as his eyes took in her bedraggled appear-ance. 'You looked in better shape when I dragged you off the road. What happened?'

'Nothing,' she answered casually, as he strode past her and flung open the door to the breezeway.

He stood quite still for several seconds, then ran a hand across his eyes as though to erase a nightmare, before stepping into the room. 'What did you do?' he asked in a voice that was entirely void of any expression. 'Make the meal and then *feed* it to the whole damn room?'

'Oh, I just knew you'd say something mean,' she wailed, 'but I'll have you know that none of this mess is my fault.' She marched over to pick up the magazine, which was now sadly splattered with all the ingredients it had told her to use. 'Whoever made up these recipes couldn't have tested them. I did everything they said, but nothing turned out the way they promised, and if the magazine wasn't so outdated, I'd write to them and complain!'

Nicholas stepped over a pot and then skidded on something brown that had dripped from a spill on the stove to settle on the floor. 'My poor wee shack,' he groaned, shaking his head sadly. 'For over fifty years it's sat here, minding its own business, sheltering people from storms, from the heat and the cold. It never cared that it didn't have electricity, or hot and cold running water, or fine furnishings. All it asked for was a coat of paint now and then and maybe the odd repair to keep it serviceable. But what does it get?' he asked, keeping up his sorrowful lament while gazing mournfully about the room, before settling on Victoria's guilt-flushed face. 'It gets a young lady who boasts that she can cook, while in fact she's tried her first ever recipe, then true to form has the audacity to blame a reputable magazine for her failure. Not only that,' he continued relentlessly, 'it looks as if she's managed to use up a full week's supply of food in the process.'

'I-I'm sorry,' she apologised, feeling miserable. 'I haven't used much of anything . . . it just looks that way,' she added weakly. 'But don't worry about the mess, I'll have it cleaned up in no time. If you hadn't barged in the way you did, you wouldn't have had to see it.'

'But now that I have, may I also remind you how long it took you to clean up from our lunch this afternoon, without any of this . . .' he waved his hand '. . . cyclonic debris?'

'You'd better be careful,' she surprised him by warning. 'After all, I haven't lost the bet yet. My offer to clean up was very generous, I thought, considering I'm cooking the meal, which I fully intend doing. You did say you'd settle for scrambled eggs, remember, so scrambled eggs it shall be.' She tightened the apron around her waist, then cleared a spot on the bench, not daring to look at him. 'Now, if you'll just tell me how you like your scrambled eggs cooked . . . I'll cook them,' she finished, swinging around to face him, an expectant expression on her face.

Nicholas leaned against the wall, his eyes mocking her, a twisted smile on his lips. 'I'll have my scrambled eggs . . . scrambled,' he told her.

'Well, I know that,' she snapped, slumping her shoulders in exasperation, 'but how do you want them cooked?'

'There's only one way to cook scrambled eggs, you idiot, you scramble them!'

'Oh!' she answered in a small voice. And then: 'Are you sure?'

'Look,' he said, taking her arm and leading her to a stool, 'you sit there and watch while I make the eggs. You know, I've heard of women who can't cook and I've even met a few who boasted they couldn't boil water, but until now, I've never actually met anyone so totally helpless when it comes to the most basic of domestic chores.'

'Well,' she protested feebly, reaching up to tuck a few stray strands of hair behind her ear, 'I feel I've done fairly well so far. If you'd had the proper ingredients in your cupboards, then I wouldn't have had to improvise so much on my recipes. After all,' she declared impishly, peeping up at him through a thick veil of lashes, 'I only did it for you, I wanted you to sit down to something really special.'

He gazed at her through narrowed eyes, then laughed, the sound coming from deep within his throat. 'I'll just bet you did!' he agreed drily, a sardonic expression in his eyes as he probed her face. 'Why?'

The bluntness of the question startled her, but not half so much as the harshness with which it was ejected from his throat. She looked down and swallowed, then gazed helplessly up at him, wondering at the cold angry glint in his eyes. 'Well, I suppose I wanted to impress you,' she answered truthfully, feeling her cheeks colour at her admission. 'I guess . . . I wanted to change your feelings towards me, make you see that I could be useful and . . . and . . . helpful.'

He let out his breath in a long, ragged sigh. 'Well, I'm afraid you've accomplished quite the reverse. Far from being helpful and useful, you've only managed to waste time and supplies. The chickens haven't been fed, we haven't eaten and it will be hours before this mess is cleared up. I was hoping for an early night, but it looks as though it really will be midnight before we can turn in, and I wanted to be away before dawn.'

'I'm sorry,' Victoria muttered miserably, getting to her feet to start clearing away the bench, while Nicholas filled a pot with water and set it on the stove. He took out a sack and she pretended not to notice while he measured out the laying mash into the boiling water. After a few quick stirs, he poured it into a tray and held it out to her.

'Take this out to the chickens. They'll be getting anxious, wondering about their tucker.'

'But I couldn't do that!' she protested, backing away from the outstretched tray. 'I don't know anything about chickens, they might bite me!'

'Chickens don't bite, they peck,' he told her patiently, thrusting the tray into her hands. 'Now get out there and feed them, while I make a start on our own meal.'

But she lingered at the door, chewing nervously on her bottom lip, while she stared helplessly down at the tray.

'Now what?' he thundered, as she made no move to do his bidding.

'I . . . I . . . was just wondering . . . shouldn't I have some sort of . . . of protective clothing? Like a hood with a veil for my head and perhaps gloves for my hands?'

'That's what beekeepers wear! You're not going out to empty a hive, just to feed a few hungry chickens. Now, will you quit stalling and do as you're told.'

'But you said they peck! They might try pecking at my eyes!' She shivered.

'God, don't tell me you're afraid of a few small chickens?' he roared impatiently, as he endeavoured to clear away the bench in order to make room for the preparation of their meal.

'Yes, I am, as a matter of fact,' Victoria confessed readily. 'Terrified would probably be even a better word.'

She waited for him to say that she didn't have to go, that she could do something else while he fed the chickens. When he didn't make the suggestion, she quietly laid the tray on the floor beside the door. Picking up a broom, she began sweeping, putting as much room between herself and the tray as she possibly could.

But before she could say 'Bob's your uncle' the broom was traded for the tray and she was pushed unceremoniously through the door, with the warning: 'You don't eat until they do and make certain you latch the gate when you're through!'

She trudged reluctantly, unwillingly through the frangipani trees, past the hibiscus shrubs, past the old fiddlewood tree, to arrive at the clearing where the chicken pen lay. The last rays of the sun shot down beyond the pen, blanketing the hills with a blood-red brilliance. The pen and the chickens it enclosed stood out as though etched with charcoal, stark, still, mysterious, much like the aboriginal sketchings of long-forgotten times.

Then, as though showing her just what it could do, the sky changed. Slowly, almost imperceptibly, it altered from crimson to deep purple with flashes of green, before fading into gradual darkness. Now only the slightest wisps of pinks and oranges lingered to remind her of what she had just seen.

The tray lay forgotten in her hands. Not until she felt it being gently removed from her grasp did she realise she had been holding her breath and that Nicholas was beside her.

She turned slowly towards him, her lips slightly parted, her eyes soft and dreamy. He put his arm around her shoulders and she fitted against him as snugly as if he had been specially built just for her.

'Beautiful,' he murmured against her hair.

'Yes,' she whispered softly. 'I've never seen anything quite so spectacular.'

'Neither have I,' he agreed, as his lips caressed her hair that had turned silvery white in the moonlight.

'We don't have anything like it in Sydney,' she told him, reaching up to place one little hand against his chest.

'Not any more,' he confirmed, his fingers resting gently against her cheek.

'Too much smog . . . pollution, that sort of thing,' she

whispered, as her hand crept inside his shirt.

'Purity is something that most of us tend to forget exists,' murmured Nicholas, as his lips found hers in a dizzying embrace. Her hand crept across his chest, to slide smoothly along his back. She forgot everything, nothing was important compared to this exhilarating experience of being in his arms, of having her whole being respond to his caresses.

His arms encircled her, drawing her nearer, crushing her against him. She felt her body moulding into his, as though the fires that raged between them had fused them into one being. His hands tore at her shirt, pulling it free from her slacks, and she felt him unclasp her bra. She gasped with pleasure as his hands found her breasts, stroking the tips until she felt them go rigid in his hands.

A new sensation swept through her body, one that was both ecstasy and torment as it flowered within her, reaching every nerve and pulse in her body. Her hands slid along his back, soft and smooth as they traced the rigid curve of his spine and then the muscled breadth of his shoulders, before snaking up on their own accord to lose themselves in the thick, luxurious mass of hair.

His lips left her to burn a trail of liquid fire across her burning cheeks, down the smooth, soft column of her throat. She felt him tremble against her own trembling body, as he slipped her shirt from her shoulders.

'Nicholas,' she gasped, as his lips bit into the soft yielding flesh. 'Oh . . . Nicholas,' she moaned, her eyes shut and her head back as she felt his mouth slip from her shoulder to her breast.

She heard him groan, a sound filled with anguish, as he suddenly released her, holding her away from him.

'Hell!' he muttered in an agonised voice, his eyes dark with passion as he gazed into her pale face. 'I'm sorry, Victoria, I truly am,' he added thickly, while he swept one trembling hand through the thick scrub of his hair.

Her own eyes were huge, almost black, as she stared up at him. A hauntingly beautiful expression masked her features, touching every curve and plane with an innocent aura of vulnerability. She reached up to touch his cheek. 'Don't be sorry,' she whispered softly, 'I'm not. And besides, we didn't really do anything that was so terribly bad.'

Nicholas took her hand and bowed his head over it, gently kissing the soft moistness of her palm. When he raised his head to look at her, her heart froze in her chest. The tenderness, the yearning and the passion had mysteriously disappeared. The moonlight cast a shadow over his eyes, making them extremely dark, mysterious. Victoria's heart sank at the old familiar expressions, as his eyes raked her half-naked body. The mocking look was back, made much worse by the potent anger that flashed from narrowed eyes.

'I promised you you had nothing to fear from me, that I'd never touch you,' he growled fiercely, making her flinch from the sheer ferocity of his manner, as he stood over her. 'Now, get back to the shack and have your dinner, while I tend to the fowls.'

As she turned to go, he grabbed her wrist. 'Make certain you're out of sight when I get back. A man can be tempted just so far!'

She wrenched herself free and ran blindly back to the shack, clutching at her clothes as she ran. Tears streamed unbidden down her pale cheeks, as great racking sobs tore from her throat.

She crashed through the breezeway, stumbling over stools and banging against the bench, in her haste to get through the room and on to her own little cot.

It seemed a long time before she heard Nicholas

return to the shack. She listened to his movements, knowing exactly what he was doing by the sounds he made. The breezeway would be spotless by morning, she knew, and she longed to go out and give him a hand, but she didn't dare . . . and besides, she knew he didn't want her to.

She heard him go out and through the thin walls of the shack she could hear water running, so knew he was taking a shower. Moments later he returned and his footsteps warned her that he was coming into her room.

She turned quickly on her side and forced herself to breathe evenly, as he stood silently over her bed. When his hand reached out to stroke her hair it was more than she could bear to keep herself from calling out.

Then she felt, more than heard, him leave and as he shut the door behind him, small tears of misery trickled from her eyes.

She rolled over on to her back. Through the small window she could see the sky. As she watched, the moon slipped out from behind a cloud and for a brief moment the whole sky appeared to frame one tiny star.

Victoria closed her eyes . . . and wished!

CHAPTER SIX

SHE sat upon a rock. The rock was grey, hard, but it felt warm against her thighs. She was looking towards the chicken pen, her eyes as grey as the rock she was sitting on and almost as lifeless.

Her heart too was like the rock. It felt heavy, hard inside her chest and it hurt. The rock inside her chest hurt so much that she felt the weight of it would crush against her ribs and she would be killed.

The only part of her body that didn't feel cold was her face. She had a fever. And the fever hurt. She had felt this way for the past few days.

Nicholas had gone by the time she awoke that morning after their mad embrace. And it *had* been mad, this she now painfully realised. He had returned by lunchtime, his manner towards her cold, but very, very, polite. He had prepared their meals, cleaned up afterwards, fed the chickens.

In the evenings he had worked on his maps, plotting out new possibilities where Dynamite might be.

He was courteous, she couldn't fault him on manners, but apart from necessary speech there had been absolutely no conversation between them. It was almost as though he had forgotten she existed.

Several times she had turned, feeling his eyes upon her, but there had been a dark censure in his eyes, grim and hard, making her shrink and shy from him like a nervous animal in the bush.

As she sat there on the rock, her thoughts turned to her father. The flood waters were receding, she would soon be home. She should be glad, but she wasn't. Going home would be trading one prison for another. She had two men in her life, and they both terrified her.

She wondered if she could bear the loneliness of her father's home after being here. She half smiled, looking about her. Except for the chickens, there was nobody else for miles and miles. She had lived in Sydney all her life, with neighbours on both sides, in front and behind, but she had never before faced up to how utterly lonely her life had been.

She thought of the board meetings—long-drawn-out, monthly sessions of formal, pompous talks. The weekly sessions in her father's office, where his top executives met to prepare feasibility studies on future land developments—she had been required to sit in on these functions, but as yet she hadn't been permitted to speak. She was still an apprentice in her father's eyes. Not until she proved herself would she be allowed to physically participate.

The purchase of Teddy Harrington's property was to change all that. She had done everything on her own; from the purchase of the mortgage to the conclusion of the final sale, and all within the strict guidelines of her father's tried and true methods of guaranteed success.

She thought of the evening at home, where the routine was always the same—home from the office at six, bathed and changed by seven, dinner at eight o'clock. She pictured what she and her father must look like, sitting at the long dining table, one at each end, hardly a word passing between them; the silent servants, stiff and formal, hovering like ghosts in the gloomy dining room, placing trays of food that always tasted the same, to pick them up later with the food barely touched.

Her father would take his coffee into the library and

she would go into the sitting room, read a book . . . and dream!

She got up from the rock and walked over to the chicken pen. If only she hadn't been so afraid that night, then Nicholas probably wouldn't have come out to see what was keeping her. But the sunset had been so beautiful, spectacular in fact, that she couldn't help but watch it.

But if she hadn't watched it, just fed the chickens as she was supposed to do, then he wouldn't have come out after her. She would have gone back to the shack, had her meal, helped with the cleaning up and then they would have gone to bed.

But there would have been that companionship in between. She loved being near him, his quick grin, the way his hair fell over his forehead when he bent over the fire. She felt safe with him. With him she had a security that made her feel protected, made her feel that she was . . . *someone*! A woman, beautiful and desirable, and there had even been moments when she had felt cherished, like in her dreams.

Nicholas had humbled her, ridiculed her and at times he had even been cruel to her. Victoria sighed and pressed her brow against the mesh netting of the pen, while her eyes filled with tears and flowed down upon her cheeks. Yes, he had even been hard on her, but she had *loved* every minute of it!

She made no effort to stem the flow of tears or muffle the sobs that escaped from her throat. There was no one to hear her cry, just like there never had been.

Finally she turned and walked towards the shack, a small, solitary figure against a lonely background.

The shack was spotless, the way Nicholas had left it. He would be home soon, and she smiled wistfully at how she had come to think of this place as 'home'. But home was where the heart was, and despite Nicholas's feelings towards her, she knew her heart belonged to him. She wasn't as naïve as Nicholas apparently thought her to be. She knew what had passed between them that night outside the pen had been unavoidable. If she lived to be a hundred, she would never forget the sweet ecstasy of being in his arms, of having his lips pressing against hers, thrilling to his touch that had left her dizzy with desire.

Nor would she forget the pain that had followed, the cold, empty ache that now seemed destined to destroy her. There was only one anecdote that could cure this bittersweet agony, and that was Nicholas himself.

But he hated her, just as he seemed to hate her father and his corporation. Victoria flopped down on her cot, a few of the old magazines in her hands. She flipped through the pages, idly, not seeing the words or the pictures that shuffled through her hands. Every now and then she sighed, a love sigh, sweet and mournful with yearning, but sad, almost pathetic with its futility. She was hooked on love . . . !

She dozed, and when she awoke she guessed it was well past noon. Nicholas was late. She ran out to the yard and peered into the direction he should be coming from, but he was nowhere in sight. As always, when he was even a few minutes past the time she expected him, she began to fret.

Worrying over someone was another new experience for her, but one she didn't like. She paced the shack like a caged animal, going from window to door, to window, to door, to outside. Time crept by like a forbidden enemy.

By late afternoon it began to rain. The odd drop at first, then changing to heavy downpours. Nicholas would be wet and hungry by the time he returned. She grabbed one of the magazines. Damn it all, anyway, she would cook him a meal and this time she would make certain it was above reproach. She threw herself into the preparations and found that she had learned considerably just by watching Nicholas.

With her stew bubbling merrily on the stove, the table nicely set, the lantern glowing cosily, she decided she would even go one step further and feed the chickens. It was a wet night and they would need their hot mash. A few minutes later, she slipped from the door and raced across the yard to the chicken pen. The rain was coming in great sweeping lashes, and the wind was howling. Victoria prayed silently that Nicholas wasn't out in this horror, but that he had found suitable shelter somewhere.

The chickens were huddled in their house, propping one another up by leaning on the other's shoulders. She scraped the hot mash into their bucket and watched while they gobbled it up.

Outside in the rain and the wind she thought she heard a roar. She stood quite still and listened again, her heart thudding in her chest. The wind continued to howl and a branch snapped from the old fiddlewood tree, landing to the ground with a terrifying rustle. Again she heard the roar, but this time she knew what it was. It was Nicholas. He must be hurt—he was shouting for help.

She raced out of the pen and ran blindly across the yard, in the direction his cry for help was coming from.

'I'm coming, my love!' she cried. 'I'm coming!'

'Victoria!' he soared. 'Victoria-a-a!'

They collided in the darkness. He grabbed her to him so frantically that she was puzzled, startled. He picked her up and ran with her to the shack, almost breaking the door down to get her inside.

He sat her in a chair and then knelt in front of her, taking her little hands in his big, strong, brown ones. He stared up at her, searching her face, then he bowed his head in her lap. 'Oh, my God, Victoria,' he groaned. 'When I came back and you weren't here, I thought . . . I thought something had happened to you!'

She smiled down at his bowed head, her look so tender and sweet that when he looked up and saw what was in her eyes, he moaned and shook his head. 'Don't, Victoria,' he uttered thickly. 'I'm not what you think I am, I would only hurt you, and I've done enough of that already. I love you, God only knows how much, but . . .' He got up and walked towards the door, his back towards her. His shoulders were slumped and she knew he was exhausted. She went over to him and took his arm.

'Sit down, Nicholas,' she said. 'Your clothes are wet, I'll get you a dry shirt.'

He smiled down at her and touched her hair. Her own clothes were drenched, but she had managed to sound accusatory when referring to his own.

'How did you manage to wriggle into my heart?' he asked her, a teasing note in his voice, but she knew he was serious without meaning to be. 'You really aren't my type at all, do you realise that?'

She cocked her head to one side and grinned up at him. 'It must have been my skinny legs that got to you,' she said impishly, 'or maybe it's because I've got such small boobs and hardly any clothing. You thought I was Little Orphan Annie, and who can resist an orhpan?'

He laughed. 'I knew I was in trouble when I realised you were using my toothbrush and that it didn't bother me.'

'Found out about that, did you?' she giggled. 'Using someone's toothbrush is the same as kissing them, you know.'

'I had a trying moment, though,' he said, pretending

to be stern, 'when I found little blonde hairs in my razor. Now that's what I would call a gross indecency!'

Victoria tapped her upper lip. 'I didn't want to tickle you with my moustache,' she gasped, shaking with laughter.

He hugged her to him, burying his head in the sweet curve of her shoulder. Her arms stole around his waist and her head lay against his chest. She listened to the frantic beating of his heart and she marvelled that he had suffered during the past days as much as she had.

Afterwards, when they both had changed into dry clothes, she made Nicholas sit down to the meal she had prepared.

'It looks all right,' he said, staring down at the stew on his plate. He bent his head and sniffed it. 'It even smells all right.'

'Well, go ahead,' she coaxed. 'Try it.'

'I'm afraid!' he said, his eyes dark with amusement. 'After the other night . . . !'

'Forget the other night,' she pleaded. 'This can be the beginning for us, Nicholas.'

He took her hand and kissed it, then looked into her eyes. 'You don't want to forget *all* of it, do you?'

Her cheeks grew warm as their eyes met and her mouth suddenly went dry. 'I shall probably never forget any of it,' she whispered huskily, as he brought her hand to his lips once more. Then as a tear fell on his hand, to glisten like a solitary diamond, he looked up and saw she was crying, her lips trembling like a small child's.

He scraped back his chair and scooped her on to his lap, rocking her gently. 'Don't, Victoria,' he said, his voice raw with emotion. 'I know I've been hard on you, but I've been just as hard on myself.' He stroked her hair with his lips, soothing her with his voice. 'For the past few days I've just been wandering around, trying to convince myself that what I felt for you was just a passing phase. I told myself that once you were on the plane back to Sydney, I'd forget about you.' He sighed, his breath warm against her cheek. 'But always you were there. I just couldn't get you out of my mind. It seemed every word, every gesture you'd made, had been imprinted on my mind. I drove myself crazy, remembering how mean I'd been to you.'

He gathered her closer in his arms, his eyes tender as he gazed into her upturned face. 'That night, when I forced you out to feed the chickens . . .' His voice trailed off and his arms tightened around her. 'You were so frightened and you looked so small walking out there with the tray in your hands that I couldn't let you go through with it. I went after you. You were standing still, framed against the sunset with the tray in your hands, like a sacrificial lamb.'

'You took the tray from me,' she said softly, her fingers gentle against his eyes that held so much pain. 'We talked about the sunset, but we were really talking about ourselves. It was a magic moment for both of us.'

'Yes,' he agreed softly, 'a rare, beautiful moment that not many get to share.'

They sat in silence then, the only sound they heard the beat of their hearts in perfect harmony. Outside, the wind continued to howl and the rain lashed against the windowpanes, but they were deaf to all that.

'Do you know what I think?' asked Victoria, suddenly sitting straight up in his lap. 'I think you're deliberately stalling so you don't have to eat my stew!'

He chuckled, repositioning her so he could eat, but still have her on his lap. 'Aren't you having any?' he asked, picking up his fork.

She nodded. 'Yes, I'm starved, but I want to watch you eat some first,' she told him, her tone slightly anxious. 'I want to see the expression on your face when you taste it.'

She watched closely while he chewed, waiting for signs that would prove it was the best meal he had ever tasted.

'Do you like it?' she asked eagerly.

'Mmm,' he answered, taking another mouthful.

'But is it good, I mean *really good*?'

'Mmm,' Nicholas answered once more, chewing away.

'Would you say it was delicious?' she asked hopefully.

'Mmm-mmm-mmm!' he mumbled, scraping the last bit from his plate.

'You brute!' she squealed, throwing a tea towel at him. 'It's darn good and you know it. You're probably jealous that I've turned out to be a better cook than you!' She looked at his empty plate, enormously pleased that he had eaten all of it. 'Tell me it was good,' she pretended to plead. 'Oh, hungry one, from the great flooded plains of Queensland's sunny coast, where it never rains and the sun always shines, please tell this poor humble servant that the meal you've just gobbled was the best meal you've ever eaten!'

Nicholas held his plate high. 'Wench,' he commanded, 'stop thy foolish prattle and fill this plate some more, for your master is starving and the first serve was small.'

'Oh, master, master!' she cried, hands folded across her breast. 'Does this mean that thou hast enjoyed thy first tiny serve *so much* that thou art *begging* for more?'

'Aye! It does mean that,' he growled, 'but it means much more. It means, my fair wench, that thou must always cook for me and for me alone!'

'*Oh, master!* Art thou asking what I think thou art asking? Art thou proposing marriage?'

'Nay, you silly wench,' he said, eyes gleaming. 'It

means thou probably took the the whole day to prepare such a meal and that I would most likely starve if thou cooked for more than one!'

Victoria laughed gleefully, not in the least offended, as she took his plate and carried it over to the pot. 'Why did you think I wasn't here when you came back?' she asked while filling his plate and dishing some on to her own. 'After all, the lantern was on and the table was set. You must have smelled the stew,' she continued, placing his plate in front of him and sitting down to her own.

Her eyes were soft as she gazed across the table at him, while the pain she had suffered still lingered there, causing purple smudges beneath her eyes. She had brushed her hair back from her forehead and around to one side, so that it hung damply over her shoulder, wetting the faded red shirt he had given her to wear.

Her face was flawless, the dark grey eyes smoky, and under the sheen of the lantern, she glowed like a pure thing, more precious than any gold.

Nicholas shrugged his shoulders and then leaned back in his chair, studying her beneath hooded eyes. She waited for him to speak, her breath coming softly between parted lips.

Finally he leaned towards her, making her heart quicken as he said. 'I just *knew* you weren't here. The lantern—the stew—none of it registered, except the place seemed empty, bare.' He pushed his plate away and stood up, startling her with his sudden movement. He glared down at her, frightening her with his sudden anger, as though he just realised that she had behaved out of turn, that she had dared to cause him unjust concern. 'What in blazes were you *doing* out there, anyhow?'

'I was feeding the chickens,' she answered simply, in a

tone that implied she always fed the chickens. 'Now, sit down and eat your stew, and stop trying to bully me!' She picked up her fork and began eating. She heard Nicholas expel his breath and it was only after she heard him take his place again at the table, that she dared peep across at him. He was waiting for her and when their eyes met, he laughed and said. 'You little vixen, you'll have me eating out of your hand next, if I'm not careful!' His eyes glittered across at her, a curious mixture of admiration and amusement. 'So you were feeding the chickens,' he said softly, shaking his head in wonder. 'You weren't afraid?'

'Of course not,' she answered casually, as though the idea of being afraid of a few chickens was an absurd and extremely remote possibility. 'We've become very good friends, the chickens and I, over the past few days. I think they quite like me,' she finished proudly.

He gave a loud snort. 'You should have fed them before it got dark,' he grumbled, 'and why in blazes didn't you think to throw a raincoat on? You were shivering when I brought you in.'

Victoria smiled a secret little smile, which did nothing to relieve the grim countenance from his ragged features.

'Oh, I wasn't shivering from the cold or the wet,' she owned mysteriously, jumping up to slice some damper from the loaf he had cooked the previous day and which she had forgotten to put on the table. 'Did you think I'd run away?' she asked sweetly, knowing full well that was exactly what he had thought.

'Typical female,' he drawled. 'It's not enough to drive a man half out of his mind with worry, but you like to examine every little detail to make certain his misery was complete.'

'I was just fooling,' she laughed, placing the damper in

front of him. 'It never entered my mind to run away, I guess I'm too much of a coward for that, with the weather the way it is.' She had decided there was no point in telling him that even though he had behaved like an unfeeling beast towards her, it was still better than being separated from him.

At the mention of the weather, however, it made them both aware of the raging battle taking place outside. Nicholas got up to open the door and she came to stand beside him.

'It looks bad, doesn't it?' she suggested hopefully. 'I suppose we'll be stuck here another week or two?'

'No, the rain has pretty well stopped and this wind will help dry up the land. It sounds worse than it is. You're not afraid, are you?' he asked, putting his arm around her and drawing her close.

'Well, maybe . . . just a little,' she sighed, snuggling against his shoulder.

'Liar!' he laughed. 'You're not in the least afraid, and you know it as well as I do.' He closed the door and gave her a swat on the behind. 'Now run along and put the kettle on and make us some tea. I'll get a fire started and we'll have it around the fireplace.'

The fire was going nicely by the time she had the tea ready and brought it into the connecting room. Nicholas was standing in front of it, his thumbs hooked into the front loops of his jeans, a melancholy expression on his face.

Victoria stood just inside the door, holding the tray but not advancing forward, reluctant to disturb him or interfere with his thoughts. He turned and saw her, a warm smile replacing the grimness as he took the tray from her hands and at the same time kicked a chair closer to the fire, for her to sit upon.

They sat in silence for a while, sipping their tea while

watching the fire and listening to the wind howling outside.

'Poor Dynamite!' Victoria fretted in a small, worried voice. 'Do you think he'll be all right in this storm?'

'I've seen him . . . twice now,' replied Nicholas, bending down to kick a log back with the toe of his boot. 'He's in great shape. The storm shouldn't bother him.'

Victoria's eyes were wide with disbelief. *'You've seen him?'* she gasped.

'Twice now,' he repeated maddenly, calmly stirring his tea.

'You've seen him . . . and you didn't bother telling me, even though you know I've had little else on my mind, other than his welfare and the fact I hold myself personally responsible for his disappearance? You can sit there calmly drinking your tea and tell me that you've seen him?'

'Yes, twice now,' he said once more. 'Actually, he's not far from here. The first time I saw him was the day before yesterday. I whistled to him and he pricked up his ears, gave me a rather disdainful glance and then went on eating. Yesterday I went to the same spot where I was before and he'd come considerably closer, so I sat down and waited to see what he would do. He didn't bolt, or seem to mind that he was being watched. I think he rather enjoyed the company.'

'How far were you from him?' she asked, excited now with the astonishing news. 'Do you think you'll be able to capture him?'

'He's up on a plateau and there wouldn't have been more than a few hundred feet separating us, but I didn't want to spook him by trying to round him up. He's been used to plenty of attention and people around him all the time, so it's my guess he's pretty lonesome by now. But he'll be somewhat skittish as I imagine he's had a few frights. There are things in this country, like kangaroos and wallabies, that he wouldn't have seen before, and which probably have terrified him.'

'So what will you do?' she asked, trying to visualise Dynamite being frightened by a few kangaroos and wallabies! 'Will you play the waiting game and see if he ambles up to you?' And surrenders himself, she added silently to herself, as memories of her terrifying ride washed over her, making her mouth feel uncomfortably dry.

'Exactly!' he announced, smiling at her. 'You have a pretty good understanding of animals,' he praised her, making her feel guilty about her uncharitable thoughts. 'I'll tell you what we'll do,' he said, leaning towards her and taking her hands. 'Tomorrow's your birthday. I've been thinking what we could do to celebrate, and now it's come to me. We'll have a picnic on the plateau where Dynamite is. It's beautiful there, so I know you'll enjoy it. There's even a pond, so we can have a swim.'

She stared at him, her eyes as bright as lamps. 'B-but how did you know it was my birthday tomorrow?' she asked, unable to contain her pleasure that he *knew*.

Nicholas chuckled, pulling her on to his lap. 'We have two calendars, one in this room and one in the other. On both you've circled the date and written in "V's Birthday".'

Her cheeks burned with embarrassment. 'I—I always do that,' she admitted ruefully. 'Of course that's how you knew, what other reason could there be?' she added, unaccountably disappointed and at a loss as to why she would be. She turned her head away, hurt at the amusement in his eyes. 'I suppose you think that I was hinting at something?'

He laughed aloud, wrapping his arms around her. 'Only that it's your birthday. You obviously wanted me to know,' he said, nibbling at her ear, 'and that's how you chose to do it.'

'No,' she said, jumping up from his lap. 'I—I thought you'd found out some other way. I certainly wasn't trying to make you celebrate my birthday with me, I don't even celebrate if myself.'

'Hey! Come on,' he urged, standing up to take her in his arms. 'There's no reason to get upset, I'm glad I'll be around to celebrate it with you.' He cradled her head in his hands, looking deep into her eyes. 'If you don't like celebrating your birthday, why did you mark it on both the calendars?' he asked gently, his thumbs caressing the smooth softness of her cheeks.

'It's not that I don't *like* celebrating my birthday,' she tried to explain, 'it's just that I never do. I—I mark it on the calendar, so I won't forget, that's all.'

Nicholas was clearly puzzled, she could see that, and she became even more upset. 'What's the big deal, anyway?' she snapped, pulling herself away from him to perch stiffly on the edge of her chair. 'I circled my birthday on your calendars. I'm sorry! I'll buy you two new ones, if it bothers you so much.'

'What's bothering me,' he said gently, 'is that you're obviously deeply hurt by all this and you've managed to make me feel that somehow I'm to blame.'

Her shoulders slumped as she turned away from him to gaze into the fire. 'I'm sorry,' she said softly. 'It seems . . . I'm always saying sorry to you.' She became silent, watching while Nicholas poked at the fire. She knew he was giving her time to regain her composure, but that he expected some sort of explanation from her.

'When you were a little boy,' she began, a shy wistfulness creeping into her voice, 'can you remember wanting desperately to become ten? You know,' she laughed a little selfconsciously, 'to be *two numbers*?'

'Not that I can remember,' he grinned, 'but obviously you did.'

'Yes, to me it sounded so grown up. I could hardly wait for the big day. Anyway,' she laughed, feeling ridiculous now that she had started, 'I missed the big day. I was ten for three days without knowing it.'

'So that's why you circle your birthday,' he concluded for her. 'So it doesn't happen again.'

'Exactly! See?' She smiled up at him. 'There's usually a logical explanation for everything.'

Nicholas shook his head. 'You poor kid,' he said at last. 'Didn't anybody think to bake you a cake, or give you a card at least? What about your father? Surely he must have given you presents for your birthday?'

'Oh, of course he did, if he remembered. But Father was, and still is, a very busy man. You can't expect him to remember birthdays.'

'Why not?' he asked, a stiffness entering his voice. 'Birthdays are very important events in a kid's life. Hell!' he exclaimed, looking down at her. 'You must have had one lovely childhood!'

'It wasn't so bad,' she shrugged, feeling uncomfortable now that she might have put her father in a bad light. 'I remember that my father was angry with the servants,' she was quick to add. 'He had Mr Burns, that's our head chef, bake me a very special cake—three tiers, pink frosting, the whole works. It was truly magnificent!'

Nicholas knelt down beside her, taking her hands in his. She wondered if he knew she was lying, and because she had lied, she refused to meet his eyes. 'I can't promise you a three-tier cake with pink frosting,' he said gently, thus confirming her worst thoughts, 'but there's no reason why a fruit damper, topped with chocolate fudge, shouldn't do the trick!'

Victoria dragged her eyes away from the fire to look

into his, half expecting to find mockery and amusement. But there was only tenderness and gentleness. She smiled, touching his lips lightly with her fingertips. 'That sounds lovely,' she whispered, leaning towards him. 'We can take it on our picnic and if Dynamite decides to join us, we'll give him a nibble.'

Nicholas drew her closer then, their lips touching with a quiet explosion. That night, she became his woman.

CHAPTER SEVEN

As dawn broke, smashing the darkness with fluorescent spears of colour like an artist gone mad, Dynamite rose like a statue from the crest of the hill, to peer disdainfully down at the tiny shack.

Magnificent in his solitude, he stood there, great head thrown proudly back, while smoky clouds of vapour shot from his quivering nostrils. Then, as though in protest that he considered visiting such humble surroundings, he lowered his head, shaking it violently while letting out a loud, disgusted snort, before galloping quickly away.

The early morning dawn caught the two in their bed, outlining their forms in a rosy hue. They were facing one another, Victoria nestled in the crook of Nicholas' arm like a small kitten, her long fair hair spilling over her cheek and resting against the black hairs of his chest. She stirred, and in his sleep he tightened his hold on her shoulder, as though reluctant to have her move even an inch away from him.

She opened her eyes and listened, positive that what she had heard was a horse galloping. Or had she been dreaming? Slowly she untangled herself from Nicholas' arms and crept softly out of bed, throwing on the old shirt, before creeping across the room to peer out of the window. There was nothing there, so she must have been dreaming, after all.

She turned back to the bed and Nicholas was awake, watching her, lying on his back now, with his hands cradled beneath his head. She ran over to him, a happy smile lighting her features as he stretched out his arms to welcome her.

He swung her on top of himself, pulling down her head to kiss her. 'Happy birthday, sweet love,' he murmured against her mouth.

Victoria answered him with a kiss of her own, losing her hands in the unruly, sleep-tousled mass of his hair. He turned her on her back, slipping the faded shirt from her shoulders and arms, baring her slender young body to his hard, muscled shape. He kissed her gently at first, determined not to rush her. His lips were a soft caress against her own, brushing smoothly over the surface, tantalising her with their potency. Her arms slid across his back and her lips left his to move along his shoulder, kissing him with a fever that made him forget to be gentle.

She felt his arousal and she arched towards him, pressing tightly against him. He slid partway off her, squeezing her thigh between his own, while his hands cupped her breasts, coaxing the rosy red tips to stand erect for his mouth to savour.

She moaned, her breath coming in fast little gasps as his hands slid along her body, awakening every nerve, exhilarating every sense, his mouth roaming from one breast to the other, until she thought she would scream out in sheer ecstasy.

She felt him move on to her, pushing her thighs apart as his hands slid under her, steadying her as he slowly entered her body. Momentarily she stiffened, expecting the same pain as the night before, but there was nothing, only the sweetest pleasure known to woman, as he brought her to dizzying heights before her whole world exploded into a galaxy of brilliant stars.

Their bodies were bathed in perspiration as they clung to one another, their breathing returning to normal, before they could bear to part. Nicholas leaned on one elbow gazing down at her upturned face as she looked up at him, her eyes still smoky with passion and her lips swollen from their love.

'How do you feel?' he asked her tenderly, kissing the tip of her pert little nose.

'How do I look?' she asked him, in a voice which was soft, but at the same time husky.

'Like a woman should look,' he smiled, black eyes gleaming, 'after she's been thoroughly ravished!'

'Thoroughly loved, you mean!' she said, touching the black stubble on his chin. 'You need to shave. Now that you've got me, you probably think you don't have to keep up your appearances.' She pretended to pout, while playing with the sharp black whiskers.

He chuckled, his lean fingers stroking the soft curve of her cheek. 'It's barely six in the morning and you're telling me to shave! You show a woman you love her and what happens? She starts nagging you.'

'You're so handsome,' she sighed, gazing up at him. 'I can hardly believe you love me, the way you say you do.'

'You can believe it, because it's true,' he told her, his hand tracing the outline of her firm, young breasts, before moving up to caress her shoulder. 'You're so delicate, so tiny that I'm terrified of hurting you.'

'Not too delicate, though, to wash dishes or scrub clothes?' she asked in a teasing voice.

He picked up her hand and kissed it. 'You're far too delicate for that,' he smiled, kissing each fingertip. 'I'll wrap you in cotton and take you out only when it suits me.'

'But you mustn't forget to feed me,' she reminded him. 'I'll have to keep up my strength, if I'm to satisfy your lust . . . I mean,' she laughed, 'your lust-y appetite!'

'Well, if that's not a hint, I don't know what is,' he groaned, getting out of bed. 'What will it be? Bacon and eggs?'

'Yes, please, and maybe some toast, some juice—and don't forget my birthday cake with the fudge icing that you promised to make.'

Nicholas picked up a pillow and threw it at her, while she chuckled with delight, thrilled with his attention and gentle teasing. He scooped her out of bed and planted her firmly on the floor. 'You're not going to lie there and watch me do all the work, surely?'

'Just this once,' she pleaded, hopping back under the covers. 'I've never had a man serve me breakfast in bed, and it looks so romantic in the movies that I'm dying to see if it really is as nice as it looks.' She fluffed the pillows and leaned against them, folding back the edge of the blanket and then the sheet, to make everything nice and tidy. '*Now*, how do I look?' she asked impishly, her eyes sparkling with mischief, but all the more appealing because of it.

'Like a little lady who knows how much she's loved,' he whispered, bending to kiss her. 'And who obviously knows how to take advantage of that love. Which do you want, little one, a lover or a slave?' he asked, leaning over her.

'I want both,' she said, her eyes misty, 'just as I'll be both to you!'

She saw the flash of anger in his eyes, even before he spoke. 'How careless of me,' he said coldly, straightening to his full height, 'to forget even for a minute that you're a Webster. No one ever finds freedom by creating a slave! I don't want a slave, I want a woman who gives herself freely, one who is free to love, not one who eventually cripples all emotions into a twisted snare of bondage.'

Victoria stared at him, her eyes wide and disbelieving as she listened to his words. 'But—but I didn't mean that the way it must have sounded,' she pleaded, as he turned and walked from her, pulling on his bathrobe..

She heard him pull out pots and pans in the breezeway and soon she smelled the odour of bacon sizzling in the pan, but she was no longer hungry, a sick, empty feeling replacing the delirious happiness that had so quickly been squashed by a few romantic—for she had thought them romantic—words.

How could Nicholas have misinterpreted her meaning of 'slave', and why throw the fact she was a Webster in her face? She had thought he was well and truly over that, that he had accepted her for herself and not merely looked upon her as the daughter of Malcolm Webster.

She shrugged into her shirt, pushing her hair behind her ears as she passed him in the breezeway on her way to the shower. When she had finished, she came back, a towel wrapped around her, her wet feet making marks on the floor as she padded towards him, thrusting the old shirt in his hands. 'Do you think you could find me something else to wear?' she asked. 'How about something bright and cheerful to lift my spirits? Black should do nicely, I think!' she flung over her shoulder, going into the other room.

She had made her bed and tidied up from the night before when he called her for breakfast. When she didn't answer and didn't front up to the table, he came to get her. She was sitting on the edge of the cot and turned away from him when he approached her. 'I'm not hungry,' she muttered, wishing he would go away. She had been fighting back tears and up till now had been successful. But she knew one wrong word, spoken by *himself*, would reduce her to a blubbering baby, and she certainly didn't want that, especially after last night and this morning.

She was a woman now, and today was her twenty-first birthday—high time to start taking control of her life and her emotions. She had been wearing her heart on her sleeve, so to speak, and obviously this had been a big mistake.

She had made it easy for Nicholas to cast her aside whenever he chose, and then when he beckoned with his little finger, she had been only too willing to race back to him.

Now that she was being honest with herself, she decided to face the obvious. The water had been receding rapidly and the ground was dry as far as the eye could see. She had been expecting Nicholas to announce any day now that it was safe for them to vacate the premises. They couldn't be too far from Teddy Harrington's property and could probably make it on foot. Even if that was an impossibility, then surely the road must be somewhere nearby where they could hitch a ride.

Although it broke her heart to admit it, she decided now that he had kept her here for the sole purpose of making love to her, and now that he had, there was nothing left to detain them. Right from the start, he had set out to destroy her, blaming her for Dynamite's disappearance and treating her like a common thief because she had purchased Teddy Harrington's property. He had made wild accusations about the Webster Corporation, insinuating that her father was dishonest, and at every opportunity he had ridiculed and embarrassed her, humbling her whenever he could.

Now the final humiliation! Pretending to love her to get her in his bed, and she had fallen for it, hook, line and sinker!

She understood now why he had made so much of her

wanting him to be her slave. He had been looking for an opportunity to rid himself of her and she had neatly supplied that opportunity. He didn't want her hanging around making a nuisance of herself. For all she knew, he probably had a girl-friend somewhere and he didn't want her bothering him, making things uncomfortable for him.

Well, she would show him that she was made of sterner stuff than he obviously thought she was. Even though she longed to go somewhere where she could be alone and bawl her eyes out, scream and howl and rant and rave, she would have to save all that for later, because right now she must pretend she didn't care he had treated her so cruelly, or that her heart felt as if every drop of blood had been squeezed from it.

Nicholas had brought her breakfast and placed it on the little table near her cot. She ignored it, along with the beautiful rose-coloured hibiscus that he had placed by her plate. When he returned later to pick up the tray, he brought with him a few articles of clothing for her to choose from.

When she heard him outside rummaging around the yard, she sorted through the bizarre range of clothing he had tossed on to the cot. Everything was too big, of course, but some weren't as big as others. Victoria finally decided to wear the worst possible things that he had provided—a hideous purple T-shirt and bright orange shorts. She couldn't imagine Nicholas wearing anything so gaudy, and when she had them on, she realised they must have belonged to travellers who had become lost or stranded as she had done and either forgotten to take all their gear along or had simply left them. She decided this because the clothes were too small for someone of Nicholas' stature. But they were clean and they were serviceable, and if she found it hard to recognise herself in such shabby outcasts, Nicholas obviously wasn't disturbed.

'Good,' he said, when she finally presented herself. 'I rather thought you'd choose that outfit. It's very becoming!'

She flicked back her hair and then hitched up her shorts. 'Well?' she asked. 'Are you ready for this picnic, or have you chosen to forget about it?' She hitched up the shorts again. Damn him saying he thought she would choose this outfit! Could he so easily read her thoughts? And now the darn things wouldn't stay up. She folded over the band, making them a little more secure, but soon as she took a step, down they slipped again.

'On the contrary, I'm quite looking forward to it,' he commented drily, watching while she wrestled with the shorts.

She was wishing she had thought to hang up her own shirt and slacks to dry last night when she had taken them off, when she spotted them on the line where Nicholas must have hung them. She flushed when she caught his mocking glance, which clearly read: I can understand why you think you need a slave to look after you, Miss Webster, as you obviously can't look after yourself!

He went into the shack, to come out a few moments later with a piece of rope dangling from his fingers. Without a word, he drew up her shorts, wrapped the rope securely around them and tied it in a neat bow in front. Next he got her a wide-brimmed hat, plonked it on her head and fetched her shoes, making her sit while he put them on.

Pulling her to her feet, he examined her critically and then with a weary sigh, announced she was ready to go.

Victoria trudged behind him while he carried the picnic basket in one hand and a rolled up blanket in the other. The hat was too big, flopping over her eyes and making it difficult to see where she was going. Several times she stumbled as she hurried along after him, but his long, easy strides soon managed to place a considerable distance between them. When this happened, she had to endure the embarrassment of stumbling towards him while he sat on the blanket roll patiently waiting for her to catch up.

'How much farther?' she gasped at last, after one of these much repeated exercises. Her face was flushed and tiny beads of perspiration clung to her upper lip, but Nicholas gave her no chance to rest, jumping up as soon as she was with him.

'Not far now,' he assured her heartily, swinging the blanket roll on to his shoulder, before stooping to pick up the hamper of food. 'See that weeping fig just over there, next to the small pond? Well, that's our destination.'

Victoria looked towards where he was pointing and groaned. 'But that looks hundreds of miles away! Why can't we stay here . . . *please*!' she begged, sinking wearily to her knees.

He pretended to consider her suggestion before shaking his head. 'No, the atmosphere isn't quite right,' he drawled. 'We need a tree and a pond.'

She watched him stroll off looking as cool and untroubled as when they had left the shack. She seriously considered staying where she was, but when a fierce-looking goanna slithered alongside her, she decided that a tree and a pond sounded very nice indeed. Besides, she was hungry and Nicholas had the food.

Drenched with perspiration, she finally staggered to the edge of the pond, soaking her head and her arms in the semi-cool water, before sitting on the bank to ease her poor aching feet into the sparkling blue surface.

'Ah, bliss!' she sighed aloud. 'Sheer bliss!'

Nicholas smiled at the picture she made sitting there in her gaudy array of clothing, the shorts billowing around her slender legs and her small, thin arms looking too fragile to support her as she leaned back on them. He finished spreading the blanket under the shade of the enormous tree before joining her on the bank.

His presence cast a shadow and she shot him a disdainful glance before moving pointedly away from him.

'Don't you want me near you?' he asked, squatting next to her while he dangled his hand in the water.

'No, I don't,' she lied, moving farther along the bank.

Nicholas chuckled, while one hand snaked out to grab the piece of rope holding up her shorts. 'Careful,' he warned, 'or I'll take back my rope!'

Like you took back your heart! she longed to say, but instead she managed a smile and said: 'I wonder if Dynamite has ever taken a drink here.'

'Probably,' he replied noncommittally, releasing his hold on the rope to lean back on his arms.

Relieved that he had let her go and wishing to keep their conversation away from themselves, she rushed on, 'I thought I heard him early this morning, but when I got up to check there was nothing there. I must have been dreaming.'

He lay back fully on the bank, his head cradled on his arms. 'You probably weren't. I've noticed his tracks pretty close to the shack. It wouldn't surprise me if he's checked us out now and then.'

'You make him sound . . . human, almost.'

'Don't ever let Dynamite hear you say that,' he mocked her with a laugh. 'He likes to think he's smart!'

Victoria flushed. 'He's not, though. He's nuts!'

Nicholas raised himself on one arm. 'What did you say?' he growled.

'I said he's nuts! Batty! Crazy!' She jumped up, staring down at his surprised face. 'His name suits him,' she lashed out, trembling with emotion and blinking back the tears that had been threatening her all morning. 'I think his evil little brain exploded somewhere between the United States and Australia!'

He jumped up and grabbed her by the shoulders, shaking her. 'What the hell has got into you today? You've been behaving like a spoilt brat all morning!'

She stared at him, eyes wide and incredulous. God, didn't he know what he had *done* to her, didn't he even realise what he had *said* to her? Her shoulders slumped under his grip and she lowered her eyes. If he didn't know, then she wasn't going to tell him. 'I-I'm sorry,' she said in a small voice. 'The sun . . . and the walk. I guess I'm tired.'

'And probably hungry,' he supplied for her, an arm draped around her shoulders as he led her to the shade of the tree.

She watched while he rummaged through the picnic hamper, the muscles of his tanned arms rippling with the movement. He was wearing the black T-shirt he had on when first she met him, along with a pair of old, faded denim shorts. Under the shade of the tree, he resembled a Greek god, his casual clothing not detracting in the least from his aristocratic good looks. It didn't seem right, somehow, that this proud, arrogant man should work for an employer, but she supposed his love of horses kept him at the Estate where he would be constantly surrounded by fine racing stock.

Dynamite! she thought. How could she have said such dreadful things about the horse? Her whole being filled with shame as she recalled her words. She had wanted, needed, to lash out at Nicholas, so she had used the horse because . . . Nicholas *loved* the horse! My God, she thought, the sudden realisation making her feel quite weak, I'm *jealous* of Dynamite!

But the idea was too preposterous. Nobody in their right mind could possibly be jealous of a horse. Or could they? she wondered, as she watched Nicholas take out a few carrots and some apples, placing them on a corner of the blanket before delving into the hamper once more. Food for Dynamite provides food for thought, she reflected idly, then had to smile at herself. Of course Nicholas would think to take along some titbits as an incentive in winning over the horse in case they came across him.

His constant worry over the horse's welfare and his endeavours to track him down had been nothing less than admirable, she had to admit, and she knew that Dynamite's worth had nothing to do with Nicholas' concern. She knew him well enough by now to know that any creature in a similar plight would have received the same devoted attentions.

As she had, she thought now, accepting the plate of food that Nicholas passed to her. She removed the tinfoil covering and stared down at the contents—her bacon and eggs that she hadn't eaten that morning, only now the bacon lacked lustre, sticking to the plate like a piece of old cardboard. The egg returned her startled gaze, staring up at her like a thing of mystery from some forgotten planet.

'Oh,' she said in a small voice. 'This looks good,' she added weakly, feeling her stomach heave in protest at the revolting treat.

Nicholas glanced at her plate. 'The egg stood up to the trip quite well, don't you think?' he asked proudly. 'I was a bit worried about the yolk . . . thought it might break, seeing that it was only lightly fried the way you like it, but then the grease cemented it down quite effectively, wouldn't you say? Of course, the tinfoil helped, kept it together instead of sliding over the plate. Otherwise it mightn't have looked as tasty as it does now, if the yolk had run all over the bacon.'

'Yes, well . . . as it turns out, your worries were unwarranted,' she replied, hating him for his nastiness and his obvious enjoyment of the lesson he thought he was teaching her.

'Isn't it always the way?' he commented drily with a shake of his head while he busied himself slicing thick wedges of ham on to his own plate which already held fresh pineapple, sliced tomatoes, potato salad, some cheese and two huge dill pickles. 'I almost didn't pack your breakfast, would you believe it, but then I got to thinking. I thought, Victoria wouldn't have asked for bacon and eggs if she had no intention of eating them, so I decided I must have misunderstood you, that you didn't want them for breakfast, you wanted them for your picnic. I made a mistake . . . silly of me, wasn't it?'

'Yes,' she muttered, poking at the bacon, 'very silly.'

'Oh well,' he shrugged, leaning against the tree with his plate balanced on his knees, 'as long as everything turns out in the long run that's all anyone can really expect.'

'True,' she agreed amicably. 'Very, very true.'

'Of course,' he continued, in easy tones, 'there's plenty of ham and salad, if you care for some.'

'No, I don't think I shall be able to eat anything, ever, after I've finished this!'

'Filling, is it?' he asked, watching her with amusement as she nibbled at the bacon and then at the egg.

'Quite!'

'It's the protein in the egg,' he assured her wisely. 'Protein is very satisfying.'

'So I'm told,' she agreed, wondering if she would ever feel the same about eggs again.

'Well, you ate that fast enough,' he said approvingly, as she swallowed the last of the meal.

'Yes,' she gulped, 'I decided speed was necessary. The flies seemed to favour my meal more than they did yours.'

'I noticed that, too,' drawled Nicholas, raising his eyebrows; 'I wonder why that was?'

She shrugged. 'Who can say, except maybe they prefer garbage to . . .' she looked significantly at his plate '. . . a banquet.'

'No, they probably just like eggs. Flies aren't very complicated, you know. I doubt if they can distinguish between banquets and garbage.'

'Well, they certainly did just now,' she grated, glaring at him. 'Do you mind if I have a slice of my birthday cake now? My mouth needs a happy ending after what it's been forced to endure!'

'Sure thing,' he agreed heartily, finishing the last of his food and putting down his plate to reach for the fruit damper. 'Pity I didn't have any birthday candles, but it still looks festive, all the same.'

'It looks . . . beautiful!' she breathed, her eyes widening in delight at the swirls of fudge, topped with candied fruit. 'Th-thank you,' she said, her hands clasped in front of her like a small child. 'Thank you very much for making it for me. I shall never forget you for this.'

She looked across the gaily decorated 'cake' to find Nicholas watching her, an expression in his eyes that brought colour to her cheeks and made her heart sumersault in her chest. Black eyes held grey in a paralysing grip that made the blood rush to her head and thunder dangerously at her temples.

His eyes caressed her face, taking in every detail from

the wide clear eyes with their thick black fringe of lashes, to her small straight nose that could at times be slightly stuck up, to the soft, sweet curve of her lips.

Victoria finally bowed her head and her hair hung around her face, giving her a forlorn, almost wistful look. His eyes had been so tender, so loving, she thought, but if he loved her, how could he possibly treat her so cruelly, humbling her by bringing along the bacon and eggs? It was true, he hadn't forced her to eat them, but she knew how he felt about wastage and the fact that she was rich. She didn't want to play into his hands by refusing to eat them. Besides, they hadn't tasted as bad as she had let on, something he had probably already guessed.

'We haven't any candles for you to wish on,' he was saying, 'but you can make a wish by slicing the first piece.'

He put a knife in her hand and then guided her, while she cut through the thick damper, the touch of his hand on hers making it extremely difficult to concentrate on a wish!

'Have you finished?' he asked, watching while a dreamy expression came and left her eyes.

'Yes,' she nodded, looking down at his hand still resting on her own.

'What did you wish for?' he asked, a mocking expression in his eyes as he took away his hand and accepted the piece of fruit damper she handed him. 'Bigger and better properties to add to the Webster Corporation?'

She laughed, biting into her own slice before answering. 'My wish wouldn't come true if I told you what it was, but if you're dying with curiosity, I'll have you know my wish had nothing to do with the Webster Corporation. At least not directly,' she added teasingly, feeling at least for the moment that she had the upper hand.

'But indirectly?' asked Nicholas, while unscrewing the cap from a large thermos and pouring out two cups of coffee.

'Perhaps,' she offered mysteriously, lowering her eyes and refusing to look at him while she sipped at the coffee he had passed her. 'When you've been brought up with something, I guess it's hard to ever dispel it from your mind completely.'

'It's always there, is it?' he asked, his lips tightening into a grim line. 'A big, gloomy shadow with you in the centre of it, never really seeing what lies beyond or even caring.'

Victoria shifted uneasily against the tree, wondering how she had lost control of the conversation and how he had managed, yet again, to see her in the wrong light. 'I'm not as self-centred as all that,' she managed to point out. 'I have interests, whether you like to believe it or not, that have nothing to do with the Webster Corporation. My God,' she spat out angrily, 'you make it sound as though we're spiders and that the Corporation is a web trapping little insects!'

Nicholas smiled, but there was no humour in the curl of his lips and his voice held contempt when he said: 'I couldn't have said it better myself! Tell me, Victoria,' he continued, as she started to protest, 'did you meet Teddy Harrington's wife when you were at their property?'

'No,' she said, surprised. 'I wasn't aware that he had a wife. The property was in his name only, so I assumed he was single.'

'Joan must have arrived back from Brisbane shortly after you . . . er . . . decided to exercise Dynamite. Pity you didn't meet her, though, she's a marvellous person. Brave in every sense of the word. She goes to Brisbane on a regular basis, but you'll have a chance to meet her when I get you back to their place. I think you'll like her.'

'Well, if she's anything like her husband, I certainly won't. I just wish I didn't have to go back there at all!' Victoria returned stiffly.

He smiled at her hot, angry face. 'Difficult to return to the scene of the crime, is it?'

'Don't be ridiculous,' she snapped. 'Why would I want to go back? I have no further business with the Harringtons. I just hope that when I collect my luggage, there won't be any unnecessary delays getting to the airport.'

'But aren't you in the least bit curious about Teddy's wife?' Nicholas continued to pressure her. 'After all, she put a lot of work into that place and she loved it. Don't you want to see what losing it has done to her?'

'What do you think I am?' she protested. 'Why must you always be rubbing my nose in the dirt?'

'You can't expect to remain immune from life, Victoria. Sooner or later it catches up with you, and if you're half the person I think you are, I think you're in for a rude awakening.'

'Oh, do you now?' she returned sarcastically. 'You think somewhere along the line I'm going to fall on my face and your only worry is that you might miss it! Well, I can assure you, Mr Nicholas Sangster, I have no intention of ever allowing that to happen.'

'You've got our roles mixed up, little one,' he drawled. 'It's *you* and your mob who enjoy seeing people lying on their faces, remember? Well then, you're in for a real treat when you meet Joan!'

'*If* I meet Joan, because right now I have no intention of even laying eyes on her. I'll do what I can to steer well clear of her and her husband.'

'That might not be as easy as you think,' he told her

curtly. 'At the very least, you'll have to spend some time at their place, and even if it's only for a few minutes, the time it will take you to grab your suitcases, I'll not have you being rude to either one of them.'

'How dare you treat me like a backward child!' Victoria bit out angrily. 'I've never been intentionally rude to anyone in my life, and I don't intend starting with the Harringtons. I was never at the ranch as a guest, I was there as a business woman, and as I've stated countless times, my business with them is completed, so I see no reason in engaging in idle chit-chat, social or otherwise.'

'Just remember what I said,' he warned her in a tight, angry voice, 'one unkind remark and I'll take you to hand personally. They've had a pretty hard run of things and they might have made it, if you people had left them alone,' he told her coldly.

'If they'd bothered doing some work around the place, perhaps they wouldn't have lost it,' she spun back. 'You're not forgetting I spent some time there, and I've never seen such disorganisation! If I were a guest, I would have demanded my money back, the meals and the rooms were that awful, not to mention Harrington's surly attitude.'

'You could hardly expect him to be a bundle of laughs, when his property had just been ripped from him!' Nicholas flung back. 'As for the meals—well, Joan takes care of that, and based on personal experience, they're excellent. Remember, she wasn't there when you were, so someone else was doing the cooking, probably Teddy, along with everything else. And I happen to know that most of their guests book again for next season when they check out, so Joan and Teddy must be doing *something* right, wouldn't you say?'

Victoria chewed on her bottom lip and looked across the pond, trying to remember a time when she had felt less unhappy than she did now. 'You care a great deal about the Harringtons,' she said tonelessly, 'I just can't understand why you didn't do something . . . anything . . . to prevent the sale going through.'

He was a long time in answering, but when he did eventually reply, it was in a voice so coldly sinister, that she felt as though he had struck her.

'I'd been away, but had I not, you never would have been allowed to stick your pretty little nose into their business, or put one dainty toe across their threshold!'

She knew he meant it!

CHAPTER EIGHT

WHEN Victoria awoke the next morning, she cast a bleary eye around the room, yawned and stretched. She was exhausted, having stayed awake most of the long night wondering if she was ever to find happiness. Or for that matter, if she was ever to have a truly happy birthday, with people who loved her wishing her well.

In one sense, her birthday celebration yesterday had been the happiest, as far as her cake and the planned activities had gone, but it also had proved the most disastrous event that had ever taken place in her entire life.

Nicholas hated her, and he had let her know just how much on her twenty-first birthday! Not only was this unfair, she had finally concluded in the wee hours of the morning, it was downright inconsiderate of anybody, telling you this on your birthday.

After Nicholas had told her that had he been around during the negotiations of the sale he would have prevented her making the purchase, there really seemed no point in continuing with the picnic. But they had gone through all the motions and from a distance it might have appeared that they were two young people obviously in love with one another and that they had escaped the pressures of the city to enjoy a quiet outing in the country where they might be alone.

That was how it might have seemed from a distance. Closer inspection would have revealed a definite strain between the two, the girl's lovely features marred by a deep unhappiness that clearly showed in the beautiful

133

grey of her eyes. The man at her side seemed like a giant compared to her frailty, alert and ready to protect or punish as a jungle cat might, his powerful muscles rippling under the deep tan of his skin.

There was something primitive in his attitude as he followed her into the pond, moving up behind her and stripping away her clothing, giving her no chance to defend herself.

He lifted her from the water and laid her on the bank. His huge hands stroked the soft white mounds of her breasts, while his mouth covered hers in a passionate embrace, stirring her to dizzy expectation, only to leave her lying there, a savage, triumphant gleam in his eyes as she lay by his feet, his for the taking.

Then he had laughed, the sound like a growl coming from deep within his throat as he turned and fetched her clothes from the water, wringing them before dropping them by her side.

She had dressed, her hands shaking as she fumbled with her clothing, her tears blinding her as she wrestled with the rope. There had been no conversation after that and she had kept her eyes averted from his grim, dark face, keeping up with him on the way back, offering no excuse or action that might provoke any further wrath.

It had been with great relief that she had finally crawled into her cot. But sleep refused to come, so she was forced to relive over and over every dreadful moment of her emotional assassination.

Now she lay there, almost numb with grief as she listened to the voices outside. Nicholas was talking with someone, the deep rumble of male voices punctuated by the unmistakable tinkle of a woman's laugh.

A woman's laugh! Victoria sprang to her feet, the covers spilling unnoticed to the floor as her brain sought to unscramble itself. But there it was again, the voices and the laughter. She tiptoed across the floor to peep out the window. Nicholas was standing there with Teddy Harrington and a dark-haired woman, their backs facing her as they examined Nicholas' jeep, which obviously had been their means of transport up to the shack.

Nicholas said something which the other two considered amusing, Teddy merely laughing, while the girl fell into Nicholas' arms in an obvious state of hysterical collapse.

Disgusted, Victoria turned from the window, then panic gripped her as she realised that naturally Nicholas would invite Teddy and what's-her-name into the shack for a coffee, or at least a cold drink. She raced over to her cot, smoothing the sheet and blanket before stripping off Nicholas' old shirt and dressing into her shirt and slacks. She had time to brush her hair before she heard the trio entering the breezeway.

Nicholas came immediately to get her, standing in the connecting doorway with a 'you'd better behave yourself' look on his face as he extended his arm, beckoning her to join him. Victoria crossed the room reluctantly, hating the idea of facing Harrington again and not at all excited over meeting the dark-haired beauty with the uncontrollable laughter.

Nicholas put his arm around her, squeezing her shoulder to let her know that he expected a smile to appear on her face. She obediently spread her lips in what she was certain was a reasonable enough smile considering her heart wasn't in it, and the fingers biting into her shoulder were really quite insistent.

'You've already met Teddy, of course,' said Nicholas, leading her into the breezeway.

She responded to the increased pressure on her shoulder by saying, 'Mr Harrington! . . . Nice to see you again!'

'And this is Penelope Winthrop, who's visiting from Perth. She likes to think she's a member of the jet-set, so she flies over several times a year to see how we're going.'

I just bet she does! 'Penelope, how nice to meet you,' murmured Victoria, stretching her lips still further.

Penelope ignored the greeting, turning to Nicholas instead. 'Really, Nicky, must you drape your arm around poor . . . Victoria, isn't it?' she asked, flashing Victoria an indulgent smile. 'I'm sure she's quite capable of standing unassisted.'

Again the smile flashed at Victoria, but try as hard as she might, Victoria couldn't get her lips to stretch further, so her clown's smile remained on her face until Nicholas looked down at her. After one more squeeze, she wiped it from her face completely, sensing his relief as she did.

'Well,' said Nicholas, rubbing his hands and looking at the group sitting around the table, Victoria nearest to where he was standing. 'How about some coffee and maybe a sandwich before we get started?'

Everyone was in agreement and Penelope jumped up immediately to help him with the preparations, while Victoria sat there stunned at the announcemnt that they were leaving. She had expected it, of course, and she knew when she saw the jeep that they would be leaving, but it still came as a shock when it was put into words. And there hadn't been any warning, no preamble leading up to the big moment, no 'Well, we'll be leaving today, Victoria. I wish it could have been longer. I've enjoyed your company and I even think for a brief moment I actually loved you. Who knows, if we ever meet again . . .' And then, of course, she might have said, 'Yes, I wish it could have been longer too and I'm sorry your love for me lasted for such a short time, but if we ever do meet again, perhaps that brief moment could stretch into a lifetime . . .'

She sighed and stirred the coffee Nicholas placed in front of her, going over imaginary conversations that they might have had. But it was probably better this way, she thought, as she watched Nicholas and Penelope. They seemed to like each other a great deal and all three of them, Teddy included, seemed to be really close friends. She was the outsider, and the smug glances Penelope cast her lay proof to that observation.

Victoria also knew if Penelope had worried about the girl who had spent a week with Nicholas in total isolation, she obviously didn't care now. Who would care? she thought glumly, admiring Penelope's exquisite beauty, while wondering if the girl was a model, with her glamorous looks. Penelope certainly didn't consider that she herself was a dangerous contender in the pursuit of Nicholas.

Several times Victoria felt Teddy watching her, and when finally she chose to meet his gaze, she was shocked at the naked misery in his eyes. He was uneasy, shifting uncomfortably in his chair, clearing his throat as though he had something difficult and unpleasant to say, but lacking the courage to say it. When Nicholas offered to escort Penelope to the small fruit grove to pick the mangoes she insisted she craved, Victoria couldn't help but wonder if the manoeuvre had been planned beforehand between Teddy and Nicholas.

When they were alone in the breezeway, Victoria kept silent, waiting for Teddy to speak. He gave one final cough, then said in a voice choked with emotion, 'When we get back to the holiday ranch, I would appreciate it if . . . you didn't say anything to my wife . . . about the sale. You see, she doesn't know I sold it and—well, I would prefer to keep it from her just a while longer.'

He bowed his head in his hands and for one terrifying moment Victoria thought he was crying, and suddenly she felt the thief Nicholas had accused her of being. But business was business, and if Teddy saw fit to keep the sale secret from his wife, that was his prerogative and had no bearing on the legalities of the purchase, since his wife's signature wasn't required.

'Well, of course I won't say anything, if you prefer me not to. It's really none of my business who you tell, or don't tell, but I think the longer you put if off the harder it's going to be on both you and your wife. After all,' she added, clearing her throat, 'you must be out in thirty days. That was part of the agreement.'

'I know,' he moaned, pushing his chair away from the table, 'I should have held out. I shouldn't have signed those bloody papers of yours—I should have had my own solicitors. Nicholas said . . . oh, what's the use?' he finished, running his hand across his eyes. 'It's probably better this way. Joan couldn't have kept up with the work much longer.'

'Wh-What did Nicholas say?' Victoria asked tentatively, tapping a nervous tattoo with her fingertips on the table.

'What?' he asked, looking up, as though through a haze, his mind, she supposed, already on another problem.

'Nicholas,' she prompted softly. 'You started to say Nicholas said something to you and then you didn't finish. What did he say?'

'Nothing that would interest you,' he said meanly, his eyes narrowing into two ugly strips.

'You . . . hate me for purchasing your property, I realise that now, but you've already admitted that it was probably for the best, that your wife found the work difficult, so why don't you just relax and enjoy the money—perhaps take a holiday or something?'

His laugh was bitter, frightening her. 'Relax, Miss Webster? How can a man relax knowing he's been duped, made a fool by a snippet such as yourself! And for the records, please don't flatter yourself into thinking you bought my place, because it was never for sale. You land developers are all the same—you see a bit of ground that interests you and presto, a mortgage is set on fire. There should be a law against crooks like you!'

Victoria's face was ashen as she stared across at him, her voice trembling as she said: 'There's no need for you to tell me what it was that Nicholas said. You've just said it for him, and it's easy to guess who's put those words into your mouth! My God, anyone would think we stole that place from you, and I've heard the assumption so often myself that *I'm* starting to believe it, almost forgetting the handsome cheque that I handed over to you and which you accepted.'

'All right, all right,' he answered wearily, rising to his feet. 'It wasn't my intention to engage in verbal warfare with you. I . . . accepted the money, because I needed it . . . badly. It seemed a lot . . . it still does, but . . .'

'But it's not nearly enough for what the ranch is worth, isn't that about the size of it, Teddy?' drawled Nicholas from the doorway. 'And certainly not enough to ever consider purchasing another property of equal value.'

Victoria spun around in her chair as Nicholas walked into the breezeway followed by Penelope. Slowly, she rose to her feet, looking from one to the other, feeling their undisguised hostility. 'Three against one is hardly fair,' she said softly. 'Teddy wasn't forced into the deal and I'm not going to be forced out if it! Nor am I about to apologise for my actions or for the Webster Corporation. Now, if everyone has said their lines, may we end this carefully rehearsed little bit of drama and be on our way?' she asked, looking coldly from one to the other.

She backed out of the breezeway and then ran along the path leading to the chicken pen. Once out of view of the shack, she slowed down until she came to the pen, her shoulders hunched miserably under the morning sun. A sound made her spin around, almost colliding into Nicholas. He grabbed her arms to steady her, but she shrugged out of his grip, her eyes blazing with anger as she glared up at him.

'You must think I'm pretty dumb,' she bit out, her voice choking with emotion, 'if you thought I wouldn't see through that little charade! You've hounded me constantly about that sale, and when you knew time was running out, you decided to confront me with . . . with a double-barrelled shotgun!'

'If by double-barrelled you mean Teddy and Penelope, then you're wrong. I had no idea they would show up today.'

'Today? So you admit, then, that you were expecting them?'

He shrugged. 'I knew that as soon as the roads were safe, someone would show up to give us a lift. We let it be known right from the beginning that we were stranded here.'

'And in this case it just happens that our rescuers are none other than Teddy Harrington, my number one enemy, and your girl-friend who likes to call you Nicky. *Nicky!* At least when she calls you that, you should have the decency to blush!'

He laughed, raising his eyebrows in mock surprise. 'Jealous, Victoria? You shouldn't be, you know. Penelope is harmless enough in her own beautiful way.'

'I'll bet she is!' she agreed wholeheartedly. 'But

you're wrong if you think I'm jealous, because I'm not. I've never been jealous of another woman in my entire life.'

'Until now?' he asked softly.

'Until ever!' she replied selfconsciously, confused by the tone in his voice. 'Anyway, Penelope isn't the issue here and we both know it. I don't know how you managed to do it, but I get the feeling that this morning was carefully planned, that you deliberately arranged for Teddy to have his little discussion with me in the hopes that I would either offer him more money to take back my agreement to purchase.'

'Suspicion follows guilt, little one,' he replied quietly. 'Teddy came here for no reason than what he told you. His wife doesn't know about the sale and he didn't want you blurting it out as soon as you got back there. He wants to wait for the right moment to tell her, maybe have an alternative property to show her to lessen the blow.'

'You never let up, do you?' she asked scornfully. 'You're wasted up here, do you realise that? With your ruthless persistence you could work for my father, he would admire your qualities, your "never say die" attitude, your inability to know when you're defeated!'

His face darkened ominously. 'Sorry, but I can't picture myself feeding off little old ladies, robbing them of home and treasures, any more than I could see myself fixing it so I could steal a man's business!'

Hurt and bewilderment washed over her, stretching her already taut nerves to such an extent that it was only her stubbornness that enabled her to remain standing facing him. 'Oh, Father wouldn't push you into sales right away,' she countered smoothly, 'that's something you would have to work up to. He'd probably start you off as . . .' she eyed him up and down, '. . . an office boy, running errands, taking messages, that sort of thing. Nothing too difficult, so it would suit you.'

Her intention had been to belittle him, to make him think she held little regard for his mental prowess and maybe, for just once, to put him on the defensive. So she wasn't prepared for his reaction. He threw back his head and roared with genuine amusement as though he had just heard and greatly appreciated, the joke of the year. Victoria stood quietly in front of him waiting for him to finish his rude laughter, while to one side she could see Teddy and Penelope standing by the jeep watching them, Penelope appearing to be undecided as to whether she should join them.

When Nicholas finally had himself under control, she said, 'You'll miss me when I'm gone. There'll be no one to laugh at!'

'I'm sorry,' he gasped, 'but you're right. I shall miss all your quaint little comments! But,' he continued, grabbing her arm as she turned to walk away from him, 'there's one more thing before we leave. Joan doesn't know who you are, so we'll keep it that way. She's under the impression that you're a guest interested in race-horses who got stranded when the flood hit.'

'I see,' she replied slowly, looking pointedly at his hand restraining her. 'No one found it necessary to point out to her that her husband tried to kill me by offering me a ride on Dynamite, is that it? Well, never mind, all your little secrets are safe with me—including my own identity,' she added bitterly.

'Don't over-dramatise the situation,' Nicholas told her quietly. 'The name Webster means nothing to her.'

'Oh, goody!' she replied sarcastically. 'Then I won't have to pretend that my name is Jones or Smith or something safe like that.'

He drew an impatient breath. 'No one is asking you to

pretend anything, Victoria. All we want to do is spare Joan the truth about the property. As you've said so often, you have no further business with the Harringtons, so let's just keep it that way.' He released her arm, regarding her for a long moment. 'It really is too bad that you aren't a Jones or a Smith!' he said deliberately, pointedly, causing a flush to creep across her face.

'This . . . Joan person . . . she must be pretty special the way everyone is bent on sparing her any unpleasantness.' Victoria remarked wistfully, chewing on her bottom lip.

'Yes, she is, actually,' Nicholas agreed with a smile. 'Joan is one of those rare, special people that come along every once in a while.'

'You obviously think a great deal of her,' she said in a low voice. 'I'm surprised you never mentioned her before yesterday.'

'There wasn't any need . . . before yesterday.'

'I see,' she replied thoughtfully. 'Joan was your trump card, is that it? Or she will be when we meet. What is she, anyway? Everyone's sister and mother all rolled up into a loving mass of humanity?'

'You might say that,' he agreed readily enough, not missing the tiny sigh that escaped from her lips.

'If she's so wonderful, I wonder why she married an idiot like Teddy?' she asked, glancing over at Teddy, who appeared to be in a world of his own, not even bothering to engage in conversation with the beautiful Penelope.

'Oh, Teddy isn't a fool,' Nicholas assured her softly. 'Nor is he an idiot. Only a Webster would mistake grief and unhappiness for incompetency!'

'Each to his own opinion,' she shrugged, moving closer to the chicken pen to peer inside. 'I . . . I'll soon be far away from here, and you and . . . and the shack, these chickens and even Teddy the lame brain,' she couldn't resist adding, 'will all just become a memory that I shall try very hard to forget.'

She trembled at the touch of his hand on her shoulder, tears squeezing through closed eyelids which she quickly attempted to brush away lest they betray her true feelings.

'Victoria,' Nicholas whispered, his voice close to her ear. 'Victoria . . . little one . . .'

'Nicky! Nicky!' called Penelope, advancing towards them. 'Teddy's getting anxious to leave, and frankly so am I. This heat is fast becoming unbearable—and don't forget Joan is expecting us, she'll be worrying about us if we don't show up soon.'

Victoria felt his hand drop from her shoulder and she leaned against the chicken pen as though her life support system had suddenly been snatched away from her.

'We'll be with you in a minute, Penny,' she heard him say, and despite her misery she had to smile at the curtness in his voice, a curtness which Penelope obviously didn't like.

'Well, really, Nicky!' she pouted. 'There's no need to snap my head off, I was only thinking of Joan.'

'Of course,' he said. 'I'll just round up a few things and then we can be off.' He headed towards the shack.

Penelope waited until he was out of earshot and then turned to Victoria. 'You've been crying,' she accused her meanly. 'Did you think a few tears would win a man like Nicholas? Well, I can tell you that the only woman who has come anywhere near winning him is myself. We're practically engaged, but I suppose he didn't tell you that. What man would, when he had a willing little shack mate to—er—bed down with, to put it bluntly.'

'Blunt is right,' flashed Victoria, feeling her cheeks

colour. 'But please don't waste time worrying or wondering about Nicholas and myself. We . . . dislike each other intensely.'

'Oh?' Penelope regarded her through narrowed eyes. 'Then why were you crying?' she demanded shrewdly.

'I . . . got something stuck in my eye,' Victoria lied weakly. 'A bit of dust, or pollen, or something. It made my eyes water. I wasn't really crying, even though it might seem I was.'

'And Nicky was trying to get it out,' Penelope concluded in a relieved voice. 'That explains why he had his arm around you—he was being helpful.'

'Yes.'

'You really should wear sunglasses,' advised Penelope, 'if your eyes are overly sensitive.'

'Usually I do,' agreed Victoria, wondering when this senseless discussion was going to end. 'But as you know, I hadn't planned on being stranded here, so all my things are back at the ranch.'

'It really was crazy of you taking that horse. You're lucky Nicholas hasn't pressed charges!'

'Pressed charges?' she gasped. 'I never would have ridden that horse had I known he was a valuable racehorse. I could have been killed! If anyone has a right to press charges, it would be me.'

But Penelope wasn't interested in this. From where they were standing, they could see Nicholas packing things in the jeep with Teddy helping him. 'Looks like they're ready to go,' Penelope remarked. 'Will you be spending the night at the ranch or will you return directly to Sydney?'

'I'll be leaving for Sydney on the first plane out. My business here is finished.'

Penelope regarded her coldly. 'As long as you realise

that!' she replied significantly, before leaving her to join the men by the jeep.

Victoria lingered by the chicken pen, reluctant to join the trio. She felt like an outsider, an enemy that had been forced upon them. Had there been an alternative way back to the ranch, she would have gladly accepted it. Never had she felt so unwanted.

Nicholas came to get her, an understanding smile on his face. 'Come on,' he said gently, taking her hand. 'The ride won't be that bad. Everyone will be too busy hanging on to pay you any attention!'

She bit her lip, annoyed that he could so easily read her feelings. Was her unhappiness so obvious, she wondered miserably, that everyone could see it?

'I wasn't worried about the ride,' she murmured awkwardly, feeling those wretched tears burning behind her eyes again.

'No?' he asked, intent interest lighting her eyes. 'Why do you look so tragic, then, so forlorn?' His hand swept the length of her smooth, blonde hair and she swallowed hard to keep her voice steady.

'I . . . was wondering about the chickens, that's all,' she managed shakily, gulping back the lump in her throat. 'You're not . . . just going to leave them here, are you?'

'For now, I am. They have plenty of food and water to last them until tomorrow. I'll send someone around to collect them then.' He gave her a questioning look. 'You're certain that's all that was bothering you?'

'Yes,' she nodded.

'Well, now that you know the chickens will be taken care of, you can stop guarding their pen and we can be on our way.' He took a few steps towards the direction of the jeep and then turned around. 'Quit stalling, Victoria,' he said impatiently, a frown crossing his features. 'These people were good enough to give up their time fetching us and I don't like keeping them waiting unnecessarily.'

'All right,' she agreed reluctantly, heading towards the shack. 'I won't be long.'

'Where are you going?' he asked, exasperation creeping into his voice. 'The jeep's this way.'

'I thought I'd better check on the shack. You know, make certain everything is all right and that we haven't forgotten anything.'

'I've checked on everything and you're already wearing your only possessions, so I doubt if you've forgotten anything,' he reminded her patiently.

'What if Dynamite comes and there's no one here?' she asked hopefully. 'Remember, I thought I heard him and you agreed he could be close by.'

'I left him a note, for God's sake!' he roared, advancing towards her. 'You leave me no other choice . . .' he added, picking her up and slinging her over his shoulder and marching with her towards the jeep as though she were a sack of potatoes.

Penelope had already taken the seat beside him in the front, so he dropped her in the back beside Teddy. As he strode around the vehicle to get behind the wheel, Penelope turned to face her. 'It's incredible what some people will do for attention,' she accused Victoria. 'I've never known anyone to behave in such an undignified manner. Really, Nicky,' she continued, turning towards him as he entered the jeep, 'it must have been unbearable for you, stranded all that time with such an uncouth ruffian!'

His short bark of laughter silenced her and she cast him a hateful glance when he said. 'Oh, I don't know, Penny. She didn't behave like a ruffian all the time. Mostly, she behaved herself and there were even times when she was . . . docile!'

Victoria ignored them both, pretending not to hear or care what they were saying. Instead, she rolled down her window and fastened her seatbelt. Nicholas turned the key in the ignition and the motor jumped to life, obviously pleasing the man behind the wheel.

'Hey, this sounds great, Teddy,' he said, half-turning towards the back seat. 'There's life in the old girl yet!'

'I detest the way you men are always referring to motors as though they were females,' snapped Penelope, giving Nicholas a baleful stare. Nicholas ignored her, choosing to listen to the sound of the motor instead.

'You must have put in a lot of time on her, Ted old boy. She must have been in pretty bad shape when the SES dragged her in,' he commented, putting the jeep into gear and moving slowly down the rugged driveway.

Teddy laughed and for a brief moment Victoria saw what he could look like when the soured mask was lifted from his face. He really seemed very nice!

'She looked like a bloody rhinoceros the way she was caked in mud! The State Emergency Service knew she belonged to you, but they didn't want to risk towing her up to the Estate with the roads the way they were, so that's why they towed her to the ranch. I told them I'd get it up to you first chance I got,' explained Teddy, and Victoria couldn't believe the relaxed manner he had when speaking with Nicholas. But then she guessed it was only natural considering they were good friends. Or was Teddy a Jekyll and Hyde? she wondered, peeping suspiciously at him through the corner of her eye.

'You did a terrific job,' Nicholas continued with his praise. 'You mentioned when you got here that you had to replace a few parts. I hope you kept track of everything.'

'It just so happens I've got the bill right here in my

pocket,' laughed Teddy pretending to look through his jeans pockets. This caused both men to roar with laughter, and Victoria found herself laughing along with them at their good natured silliness.

But Penelope was bored with so much foolishness, letting them know this important fact by making no attempt to stifle a series of yawns coming in quick succession. Nicholas caught Victoria's eye in the rear view mirror and gave her a conspiratorial wink. She blushed and looked shyly across at Teddy to see if he had seen. He had, and half smiled at her, a smile which she found herself returning. Suddenly, *she* was part of the trio and Penelope was the outsider!

There wasn't much conversation after that, Nicholas requiring all his concentration to keep the jeep on the road. Potholes, fallen logs, stray cattle and families of kangaroos all contributing to a bumpy, nerve-racking journey.

Several times Penelope almost landed in Nicholas' lap, whether by design or accident Victoria couldn't be sure, but once when Nicholas stretched his arm around her to steady the poor girl, Penelope cast her a triumphant glance. After that, Victoria considered all future movements were by design!

It seemed to take forever before they finally found themselves on a smoother stretch of road leading to the ranch. There was no way in which Victoria could judge how far the shack was from the ranch, because they had had to take several detours. She was certain every muscle, bone and joint had been thoroughly manipulated by the bouncing, bumping and jostling she had received during the journey, however. When the jeep finally came to a halt overlooking the ranch, it was several minutes before her ears could cope with the quietness of the stilled motor.

All four of them stared at the scene several feet below them, Victoria and Teddy leaning forward over the front seat. There seemed to be people everywhere, swarming over the grounds. Tents were set up like small communities and there were caravans of every size and description. The parking area which had been designed to accommodate maybe thirty cars had spread over the landscaped grounds, and Victoria guessed there must be at least a hundred cars parked there.

People strolled in and out of the ranch house as casually as if they owned it, and along the wide verandah stretching the whole length of the building, young mothers sat holding their babies while toddlers played at their feet.

A troop of young Boy Scouts with their leaders were at the bottom of the garden, closest to where the jeep was parked, and these young heroes, for that was what they must have seemed to the mothers whose children were being entertained, organised and were supervising various games. Farther over and under a clump of shade trees, four touring buses stood.

"Wh-What happened?' was the only thing that Victoria could think to ask. 'Where did all the people come from?'

'Tourists!' explained Nicholas, slipping the jeep into gear again. 'All stranded when the flood hit.'

'It's been like this for over a week now,' said Teddy grimly. 'They just keep coming and coming, and Joan won't hear of turning any of them away.'

The bedlam, for it could only be described as such, was much worse the closer they got to it. Babies were crying, children were screaming and disgruntled adults were complaining to their tour guides, and when the jeep had stopped and they climbed out, Victoria actually heard one old couple blaming their bus driver for the flood!

Amidst all this chaos, one figure stood out. She moved quietly amongst the people, stopping to reassure them, her face kind and understanding as she listened to their complaints. Children raced after her and she would stop and talk to them, her face lighting up when one small child reached up to grab a kiss.

Victoria didn't need to see the tender love on Teddy's face or the quiet admiration in Nicholas's eyes to know who this woman was. She was Joan, Teddy's wife, her small, wasted legs covered by a blanket as she wheeled herself towards them, a radiant smile on her face ready to greet her husband.

CHAPTER NINE

Two hours after having been introduced to Teddy's wife, Victoria finally found herself alone in the room she had first occupied upon her arrival at the guest ranch. She had tried unsuccessfully to reach her father and was assured by his secretary that he would ring as soon as he returned to his office.

She treated herself to a long, luxurious bath, using the special soap she had brought with her from Sydney, and shampooed her hair with the extra-mild shampoo her hairdresser had recommended, along with her own personal tried and true creme hair rinse.

Now she sat in front of her dressing table smearing a rich moisturising lotion on to her skin, which by now had developed a beautiful honey-coloured tan. Her nails badly needed a manicure and some polish so she did this, not forgetting her toenails.

She slid open the door to the wardrobe and took several minutes deciding what to wear. It was wonderful having so much to choose from after wearing only her shirt and slacks and the old shirts Nicholas had given her, for so long.

She finally decided on a pale blue sleeveless dress, which complemented her long, blonde hair and brought out the healthy glow of her tan. She had a glow, a sparkle in her eyes that she had never noticed before, and she leaned closer to the mirror to see if it was really there or if she was imagining it. It was there, and she knew why it was, the memory of herself in Nicholas' arms bringing even more colour to her cheeks.

A tap on her door made her start guiltily, as though

through the door someone had actually seen her admiring herself! 'Yes?' she called out, moving away from the mirror to stand instead by the window.

'May I come in?'

Happily she hurried across the room to fling open the door. She didn't need to ask who it was; she would recognise that deep, melodious voice anywhere.

'Nicholas! Of course you can come in.'

He had showered, shaved and changed too, she saw, admiring him in cream-coloured slacks and chocolate brown silk shirt. She laughed and twirled around the room.

'Don't we look a treat?' she sang gaily. 'Both of us looking like human beings for a change!'

He smiled, watching her. 'All dressed up for lunch, are you?'

'Of course! Aren't you?' she asked reasonably.

'No, I had a quick snack in the kitchen which I made myself. I fixed you a sandwich. When you're ready, you'll find it on the long counter in the kitchen.'

'In the kitchen? But why not in the dining room? You certainly don't expect me to eat in the kitchen with the help, do you?' she asked incredulously.

'Why not? They're people, human beings, same as you. You certainly don't expect to be waited on, do you?'

'Of course I do. I'm a guest, a paying guest, and as much as you enjoy insulting me, I refuse to eat in the kitchen.'

'But you've seen the situation here. You must realise Teddy and Joan can't possibly cope with another guest,' he said, his voice sharp and edged with fury.

'But they have plenty of staff, and most of the flood victims are looking after themselves. They have tents and . . .'

'And rely on the Harringtons for practically every-thing, from milk for their babies, to bandages for their toddlers. Neither Joan nor Teddy have eaten a meal sitting down together for over a week, and the most sleep either one has had at a stretch is four hours. Instead of expecting them to wait on you, why not see what you can do to lend them a hand?'

'Lend them a hand?' she scoffed. 'What could I possibly do? Besides, I'd only be in the way. I know from experience that staff members prefer . . .'

'They're not staff as such,' Nicholas cut in drily. 'Most of them are locals called upon to help in emergencies. Joan and Teddy consider themselves lucky that they were able to recruit as many as they did, which happens to be the princely total of five extra workers. This isn't the only resort to be affected by the flood, you know. Every establishment for miles around is in similar cir-cumstances and most of them have called upon family and friends for assistance. Even,' his eyes slid over her consideringly, 'some of the more, shall we say, *unselfish* guests have lent a hand.'

'Don't rub it in,' Victoria murmured weakly, feeling ashamed of the time she had spent on her bath and manicure and then dressing with such care to look fashionable while she lunched in the dining room. 'I never realised . . . I mean . . . I thought,' she shrugged her shoulders helplessly, 'I thought everything was under control. It never occurred to me that I should help,' she admitted truthfully, her eyes filling with despair as she glanced up at him, knowing what he must be thinking of her.

But there was no censure in his eyes, only a grim tolerance which somehow was far worse, she thought, than any blame or disgust that she might have seen there. Obviously, by the manner in which he was regarding her, she had only behaved exactly as he thought she would.

'No one is expecting you to wash dishes or scrub floors,' he replied in an even voice, 'and I would be the first to suggest that you have nothing to do with the meals! But there are areas where you might be of assistance. You could do some of the fetching and carrying that Joan has been doing, like filling up babies' bottles, distributing extra blankets and pillows, handing out magazines, that sort of thing, simple in itself but exhausting and time-consuming when the requests are endless. Guests can be very demanding, you know,' he added, opening the door to leave, 'and selfish!'

He left, leaving her feeling rotten, in his wake. But she was determined to do all she could to help Joan, not to prove to Nicholas that she really was a caring, thoughtful person, but because she now knew the true situation was now only too glad to be of assistance in any way she could.

She picked up the phone on her night table, and after requesting and receiving an outside line, dialled through to the airport. After several minutes of discussion, she finally finished her call with the knowledge that owing to overcrowded conditions on all outgoing flights to the south, she would be unable to fly out of Cairns for at least another few days. The airports were experiencing their own difficulties with people caught in the floods and wanting to cut short their holidays.

Victoria left word with the girl on the switchboard that she was expecting a call from her father and that she wouldn't be in her room, but would be somewhere on the grounds, if the girl could manage to page her somehow.

With that bit of business out of the way, she turned once more to her wardrobe. If she was going to fetch and carry she had better dress for it. Slipping off her lovely dress, she changed into a pair of pink cotton dungarees, topped them with a pink and white striped T-shirt, pulled on a pair of white sandals and after grabbing her hair and twisting it into a long braid to hang down her back, was ready to do battle with babies, bottles and blankets!

Outside her room, she ran into Penelope loaded down with fresh towels.

'Well, take a look at you!' gasped Penelope, peeping over the top of the towels. 'It's easy to see who's the favourite around here! Would you mind opening that door,' she pleaded, nodding her head towards a door marked 'Linen', 'so I can get rid of these towels?'

Victoria did as she was bid and helped Penelope stack the fresh towels into the almost empty linen cupboard. When they had finished, Penelope leaned against the wall and very dramatically mopped her brow, a brow which as far as Victoria could see was far from damp.

'Would you believe that man!' moaned Penelope. 'He says we should all lend a hand, that Joan and Teddy need help. Fair enough, I said, never dreaming for an instant that he meant *me*! So he assigns me to laundry duty! *Laundry duty*, of all things!'

Victoria swept her hand up to cover her smile and also to smother the giggles that were threatening to gurgle from her throat. Poor Nicholas, she couldn't help thinking, to be loaded down with *two* helpless females!

'Don't feel too badly,' Victoria attempted to soothe her. 'He's got me working too.'

'You?' spat out Penelope. 'But I thought you were leaving.'

'I thought so too,' agreed Victoria, 'but I can't get a flight out. It seems even standbys are thirty thick at the counter and will be for another few days. So it looks like

I'm here for a while longer,' she finished, smiling cheerfully.

'Oh, I see,' replied Penelope, without spirit. 'And what duties has Nicky assigned to you, then? Chambermaid?' she asked, with a meaningful twist to her brows.

'Nothing quite as glamorous as *that*, I'm afraid,' replied Victoria, deliberately ignoring the intended barb. 'I'm the fetch and carry girl.'

'The what?'

'Fetch and carry. You know . . . fetch this, carry that. Fetch and carry.'

'Yes, well . . . it sounds easier than the laundry,' grumbled Penelope, as Victoria walked with her down the remainder of the corridor.

'But surely you don't actually wash the stuff?' suggested Victoria, remembering with a shudder her own stints at the laundry bucket. 'They must have machines.'

'Don't be absurd,' commented Penelope. 'Of course I don't wash anything. My job is to stack the linen cupboards with the clean laundry—such drudgery, you wouldn't believe! The muscles in my arms are aching already and I've only stacked two cupboards.'

'You poor thing,' murmured Victoria, hiding another smile behind her hand, and wondering if this was how she had sounded to Nicholas when first she arrived at the shack. God!

From the recreation room they could hear loud, complaining voices and both girls hurried their steps to see what was happening. The elderly couple Victoria had heard complaining to the bus driver, blaming him for the flood, were now having a go at Joan, who was patiently listening to their complaints. The abuse which Joan was forced to endure seemed endless, as the man and woman took it in turns to blame her for everything, from the noise the parrots made up in the trees, to the full moon which had prevented them getting any sleep the last two nights! They were bored, restless and worried, the strain on their faces only outmatched by the dreadful strain on Joan's pinched features.

Victoria listened, feeling there must be something she should do, when the elderly couple were suddenly joined by a few of their comrades who were only too eager to outdo one another in a fresh series of absolutely ridiculous and petty complaints. Victoria saw that Joan's hands were trembling and she saw red, charging into the group like an enraged bull. 'Stop this!' she ordered, in her best 'Webster' fashion. 'All of you . . . you're behaving like small children, like bullies in a school playground! This woman didn't have to open her doors to you offering you her facilities, but now that she has, I suggest you start behaving yourselves before you make it worth her while to *start charging you*! Yes, that's right,' she continued, fixing each and everyone of them with a 'no nonsense' glare. 'You might not be residents as such at this ranch, but you are using the facilities and making a lot of extra work which these people have to pay staff to provide. Now, if you have any more complaints, you must take them to . . . to . . .' she looked around the room, at the startled faces of the guests, to the disbelieving, shocked face of Penelope, 'to Miss Penelope Winthrop, who is the new programme convenor and who will also be in charge of any difficulties you might be experiencing.'

Without giving anyone a chance to regain their composure, she grabbed Joan's wheelchair and whisked her out of the room, shutting the door firmly behind them.

'Oh, Victoria thank you for what you just did! I've been dying to say it myself, but you really shouldn't have. I mean, Penelope of all people listening to their complaints!'

'And being their social convenor! They'll have all-night sessions trying to outdo each other. That will be their fun!'

Joan turned around and caught Victoria's eye, and Victoria had to give up pushing the chair as they both collapsed in helpless laughter. When they had finished and dried their eyes, Victoria asked the directions to Joan's room. 'I'm putting you to bed,' she told her firmly, 'and no ands, ifs and buts. You're exhausted, and I shall have no one to share a joke with if you collapse.'

But Joan offered no resistance and Victoria wasn't expecting any. She had seen exhaustion on her father and knew all the signs. She quickened her pace, a worried frown appearing on her forehead as Joan slumped in her chair.

Once in Joan's room, she quickly pulled back the covers and then helped Joan from her chair. She was shocked by the frailty of the tiny body as she easily lifted and gently laid her on the bed. She stayed with her until she could be certain she was resting without any difficulties and then crept softly from the room.

'What were you doing in there?' Teddy shocked her by demanding as she quietly closed the door behind her. His eyes were narrowed suspiciously, his face flushed with rage as he regarded her.

'I wasn't searching the room or stealing anything, if that's what you're thinking,' Victoria returned scornfully, brushing past him. But he wasn't to be put off so easily.

'No?' he rasped, grabbing her wrist. 'Then why were you in my wife's and my private quarters?'

'What's going on here?' growled Nicholas, coming up behind Teddy, giving each of them a questioning look.

'I just caught her coming out of our room,' declared

Teddy triumphantly. 'I told you we couldn't trust her!'

'Well?' demanded Nicholas, searching Victoria's flushed face. 'Is that true? Were you in Teddy's room?'

'Yes, I was,' she admitted quietly, a defiant tilt to her chin.

Nicholas sucked in his breath while a murderous look appeared in his eyes.

'Why?' he demanded curtly, the single word exploding like buckshot in the tense atmosphere.

'I was helping Joan get into bed. She was exhausted and she needed rest.'

Nicholas let out his breath in a long relieved sigh. Teddy appeared uncertain, but dropped her wrist to open the door. Both men peered in, to see Joan sleeping soundly on the bed, a soft breeze making the curtains billow slightly against the shaded windows. When they turned to face Victoria she had gone.

Nicholas caught up with her farther down the corridor. 'Don't judge Teddy too harshly,' he told her. 'You can see the strain he's been under.'

'That's his excuse, but what's yours?' she bit out. 'You were only too eager to believe the worst, but don't bother apologising, I'm getting quite used to being regarded with suspicion.'

'I wasn't going to apologise,' he told her patiently. 'If you insist on placing yourself in awkward situations, then you must be prepared for the consequences. But Teddy's glad you got Joan to rest and he's decided to have a nap as well. When he's rested, I'm certain he won't waste any time asking your forgiveness.'

She shrugged. 'I'd prefer if he didn't. I'd sooner see the matter dropped. Now, if you'll excuse me. I have work to do. I'm the fetch and carry girl, remember?'

'Not any more, you're not,' said Nicholas with a

laugh. 'Penelope's come up with a brilliant scheme of catering to our guests. She's appointed herself social convenor, and the idea's caught on like wildfire! She's handling all complaints, and now that the guests have their own private sounding board, they're coming up with solutions to their problems which should greatly minimise all the fetching and carrying they've expected.'

'How terribly clever of Penelope to come up with that idea all on her own,' murmured Victoria, managing a smile.

'I thought so,' agreed Nicholas, black eyes glittering as he studied her. 'But now she'll be too busy to hand out the clean linen, so I thought . . .'

'You thought perhaps I could do it,' she finished for him.

'Exactly!' He ginned, his well shaped mouth a mocking curve as he leaned towards her, causing her heart to miss a beat. 'But that won't take up much of your time, and they're short in the kitchen. You might not be a great cook, but you must know all the little touches that can turn a drab meal into something special. You know,' he continued softly, deliberately baiting her, 'a touch of the old Webster know-how. A sprig of parsley here, a sprinkle of chives there.'

Victoria ignored his mocking tones. 'Wait till I catch my breath!' she pretended to plead. 'It's hard on a girl to be handed so many responsibilities and all at the same time, not to mention being promoted from chief runner to chief cook!'

'H-o-l-d on,' he growled, giving her the satisfaction of seeing his brows lifts in horror. 'I never said anything about *cooking*! You're only to add the garnishes, make the meals look attractive. Their regular chef won't be here for the next few days and his replacement cooks well enough, but I'm afraid her meals are rather on the plain side. They need dressing up.'

'All right,' chuckled Victoria, 'I'll be glad to do it, but what has first priority? The linen or the celery curls?'

He smiled. 'Lunch is finished, but you'll be needed in the kitchen around four this afternoon.' He glanced at his watch. 'Have you had lunch yet?'

'No, I haven't,' she admitted.

'Well, if no one has thrown out that sandwich I made you, you'd better eat it now. You'll only just have time to distribute the linen, before you report to the kitchen.'

'Yes, sir. Aye-aye, sir. Anything else, sir?'

'Yes. That outfit you're wearing—it's real cute!'

'Oh, thanks,' she replied uncertainly, pleased with the compliment but suspicious of the intent behind it.

'But it's hardly the thing to wear in the kitchen. I think a plain dress, something like you had on earlier, might be more the ticket.'

How dared he! 'You mean the blue one I had on when you came to my room? That one?' she asked sweetly.

'Yes, that would be it.'

'I bought it just before I left Sydney and I haven't had a chance to wear it yet. At two hundred dollars, I was rather hoping for a more glamorous background than a kitchen, but if you think it would be just the thing, then I'll take your word for it. After all,' she enjoyed adding, 'as the spoilt daughter of a wealthy business man, I can easily buy another, if that one gets ruined with grease.'

'I'm sure you can,' Nicholas agreed with a sudden frown, 'but I think you've chosen to misunderstand me . . . yet again! The reason I've suggested something a little more formal than what you're wearing now is because it suddenly occurred to me that you would make a gracious hostess, an added attraction in the dining room. Your kitchen duties will mainly be overseeing what the others are doing. I thought you understood that,' he said, deliberately patronising her, Victoria's control snapped.

'The only thing I understand is that you're being unnecessarily domineering and overbearing, and frankly I'm sick of it. Just who do you think you are anyway, ordering people about, assigning them duties, telling them what to wear? I know you feel you've shamed me into helping Joan and Teddy, so it will come as a shock to know that I want to help them . . . Joan anyway, so it's Joan I'll take my orders from, not you!'

Nicholas chuckled, not at all perturbed by her outburst, which enraged her further.

'Why are you still here anyway?' she demanded furiously. 'Don't you think it's high time you returned to your job at that Estate you work for, or do you think you're indispensable, not in jeopardy of losing your job?' she blazed, detesting his smug arrogance.

'I'm sure my absence will be excused, when this little matter of the flood is taken into consideration. But if your concern is genuine, as I'm sure it is, then you'll be happy to know that I've rung the Estate and have received full pardon.'

'What about Dynamite, then? Why aren't you out chasing him instead of worrying about putting us through our paces? And another thing, while I'm at it,' Victoria continued, wagging her finger at him, 'I don't want to hear another word about my shortcomings, if they *are* shortcomings. The reason I'm unable to cook and sew and wash clothes is that I was never taught, and the reason I was never taught is simply because my father felt there were other more important things for me to learn. So stop ridiculing me, do you hear? I'm sick of it!'

'My, my, my!' he sighed, spreading his hands in a hopeless gesture. 'Just when I thought I had you tamed, you put me off guard by throwing a little temper tantrum!'

'That was not a temper tantrum, I can assure you!'

'No? Amazing,' he drawled, his reflexes lightning-quick as he caught her hand that had shot out to strike him.

'Words I can handle,' he said softly, drawing her close so that their lips were only inches apart, 'but I don't know how I would react to a blow!'

'Oh, I'm sure you'd think of something!' she cried, her voice almost a whimper as she struggled to free herself, while at the same time desperately determined not to drown in the hypnotic potency of the black pools of his eyes, as he smiled down at her.

She was well aware of his intent even before she saw his head dip, his lips claiming hers with a ruthlessness and brutality she had hitherto never experienced. Savagely his lips bit into her own, forcing their tightness apart as his arms clamped around her, pinning her softness against the hard wall of his body. Even as she struggled she felt the fires of passion consuming her, weakening her pitiful resolve not to succumb to him, the wild throbbing of her heart frightening her, as she surrendered at last to the exquisite pain of his cruelly possessive embrace.

'That's better,' he murmured against her lips, smiling while she stared up at him, her eyes dark and cloudy with desire. 'No more tantrums, no more punishment! If you insist on behaving like a wildcat, my little love, then you must be prepared to be treated like one!' His fingers slid around her throat and then up to brush across her lips.

Somewhere a door slammed, the sound reverberating

in her brain and mercifully releasing her from the hypnotic state that Nicholas' eyes always seemed to hold for her. She backed away from him and he let her, his arms sliding down her back in a last caressing embrace. She half crouched, facing him, her trembling hand strange against trembling lips. Her whole body was trembling, she realised with dismay as one hand crept up to her breast to feel the dangerous throbbing of her heart.

'I hate you!' she managed at last, her voice a hoarse whisper in her throat.

'Sure you do,' he growled mockingly. 'Like a bee hates honey!'

Tears of anger and humiliation sparkled in her eyes.

'You're cruel . . . heartless!' she moaned, putting her fingers up to her raging temples.

He shrugged, eyes as hard as flint as he said, 'That makes two of us, then, as I'm sure that's how Joan will view you when she finally learns . . . what you've done to them!'

As sudden as her anger had been to spark within her, it died, leaving her feeling helpless and defeated, totally void of any vitality. She raised her hands, then dropped them like dead weights at her sides. He laughed, the sound low and sinister to her ears.

'Caught in your own web, Charlotte?' he threw at her, before turning on his heel to walk away, leaving her alone . . . *all alone!*

She avoided him after that, just as surely as if he had the plague. Her only salvation, she knew, was to make herself as inconspicuous as possible, going about her work and minding her own business much like their servants at home.

In fact she copied them, assuming their manner, adopting their silent attitude as she went about her daily chores. She became her own boss, quietly criticising herself for any job that was done without perfection, shining or polishing or scrubbing until at last she had received her own approval.

She drove herself relentlessly, finishing one job only to find another. She worked in the kitchen, in the storerooms, in the laundry. She set and waited on tables in the dining room, served behind the bar, washed glasses, shined glasses, stacked glasses. She cleaned all the brassware in the rumpus room and rearranged the furniture in the huge lounge. At night she babysat for young couples, giving them an opportunity to take part in the evening activities.

Most nights she didn't crawl into bed until after twelve, setting her alarm for five the next morning. She was always the first in the kitchen, setting the huge pots on to the stove to boil the water for the porridge. Then she would nip out into the garden to pick fresh flowers, arranging them into vases to place on the tables.

And while she drove herself, Nicholas watched, his eyes quietly brooding as he traced her every step, studied every movement. Victoria knew he watched her and she became even more determined that he mustn't find fault. She worked harder, faster, finding more and more chores, lest he discover one that she overlooked.

She lost weight and became pale, hardly ever taking the time to sit down to a decent meal and always refusing to eat with the Harringtons knowing that Nicholas and Penelope would be at the same table.

She deliberately avoided putting on make-up and she wore her beautiful hair in a bun behind her head. It was all part of her punishment, and she told her father on the phone that she was seriously considering becoming a nun! He told her he was too old to care what she did, so Victoria sank further in her misery, wondering if it was possible to become obsolete when you were still alive.

By the end of the week the roads became almost passable and the guests began to celebrate, knowing their enforced stay was soon to end. Penelope was in her glory, planning games and special dinners, and Victoria willingly became her slave, making party hats, special 'Who Am I' tags and all sorts of silly things that, judging from the laughter that drifted into her room until the wee hours of the morning, must have been highly successful.

As Victoria's misery grew, ripened and perfected, so too did Penelope's happiness. She no longer considered Victoria a dangerous contender in the pursuit of Nicholas, and if the knife was twisted a little more deeply, a little more painfully into her heart, Victoria never let on that it was killing her to see Penelope snuggle up to *her man*, to watch with tears in her eyes as Penelope danced with *her man*, or when Penelope shared a secret with *her man*!

Throughout all this misery and heartbreak there was always Joan. Joan with the quiet, sad eyes, as she wondered at her husband's unhappiness. Joan, who was always there to lend a hand to a dispirited guest. Joan, who was deeply worried about Victoria, begging her to slow down, asking, always asking if there was something she could do.

Joan and Nicholas! Nicholas and Joan! Their eyes haunted her in her sleep, turning every dream into a nightmare. She was going mad!

Gradually the guests began to leave. They left in groups, at first, the more adventurous leading the way and ringing up along their route to tell the others about the roads. Victoria waited for Nicholas to go, certain that he must be concerned about his job and eager to be on his way.

But as the guests became fewer and fewer and still he made no signs of departing, taking leisurely strolls with Penelope around the gardens, she wanted to shout at him: 'What about Dynamite? Have you forgotten about Dynamite? Remember, it was *me*, Victoria, who took him that day. Have you forgotten? Have you? Have you?'

'Pardon me, Miss Webster,' a voice beside her said, and she turned from the window to find the young man who had spoken to her on several occasions during the week, standing by her side, a sheepish, embarrassed expression on his face.

'Y—Yes?' she asked, trying hard to smile for his benefit because she knew how shy he was.

'You mentioned a while ago that you live in Sydney and that you were waiting for a flight. Well, I've just rung the airport and, as luck would have it, there are a few seats left, so if you care for a lift, I can drive you there, but we'll have to leave immediately. The flight leaves in one hour.'

Victoria stared at him, trying to unscramble the message her brain had just received. A flight. To Sydney. Leave immediately.

'Yes. Thank you. I've only a few things to pack.' She left him standing by the window as she raced down the corridor. Once in her room, she pulled her suitcase from the top shelf of her wardrobe, grabbing her clothes from their hangers at the same time. She stuffed them into her case, forgetting about her toiletries in the bathroom. An hour, he said; they would probably just make it, and with Nicholas out in the garden and Joan taking her nap, there would be no awkward and painful goodbyes. She would leave as she came, unheralded, unannounced and unloved. Nothing had been lost, she told herself, and nothing had been gained. Tomorrow she would be back in Sydney and it would be business as usual.

But today . . . now . . . there was something she must do.

CHAPTER TEN

VICTORIA grabbed her briefcase and after unlocking it, drew out the contracts for sale that Teddy had signed. Without any hesitation she ripped them up, tearing them into small pieces before placing them into an envelope, which she sealed and then scrawled his name across the face of it.

This done, she felt happy, peaceful in the knowledge that without the contracts duly signed by Teddy, there could be no sale. The ranch was still his.

With one last look around her room, she blinked back tears while she picked up her suitcase, her briefcase and the all important envelope. She would place it on his desk in his office, and by the time he discovered it she would be on the plane back to Sydney.

The corridor was very quiet as she crept softly towards Teddy's office. Outside his office she listened at the door, her heart beating wildly in her chest as she thought how it would look if anyone happened to pass by now. There were no sounds coming from within, so she quietly opened the door, hurried across to the desk, placed the envelope against his desk calendar where he would be sure to spot it and then quickly turned to leave.

As she past the window in Teddy's office, she saw Nicholas speaking to Graeme Muir, the young man who had offered to drive her to the airport. For a second she panicked, terrified that Nicholas would remain speaking to Graeme until she joined them by the car. The idea of having to say goodbye to Nicholas, the man she loved and would always love, was too much for her to bear.

She just wasn't up to facing the contempt and hatred in his eyes and voice as he bade her farewell.

She glanced at her watch. There wasn't time to spare if they were to make that flight. What could they be discussing? she wondered nervously as Nicholas glanced up at her bedroom window. Even from this distance she could see the loud, angry look on his face as he turned back to Graeme Muir. Then to her astonishment, Graeme got into the car and drove off.

Drove off? Now what was she to do? Without thinking of the possible consequences, she flew out of Teddy's office, stopping only long enough to pick up her bags which she had left outside the door and then raced along the corridor. Somehow she had to wave Graeme down, catch his eye, do anything to attract his attention and make him stop. She couldn't, just couldn't stay here another instant. Why on earth had he left without her? Had he told Nicholas that he was waiting for her and had Nicholas made him leave? She knew it was highly possible. Nicholas probably had more punishment in store for her, thinking she hadn't quite suffered enough!

Well, she would outsmart him. He was probably on his way to her room now, thinking he would catch her in the act of packing and that he would have the opportunity of placing a few nasty insinuations in her direction, humbling her and hurting her.

Instead of turning towards the main lobby, she continued straight, along the corridor leading to the Harringtons' private quarters and on through to their secluded patio. Beyond that were open fields where if she hurried she should be able to flag down Graeme's car as he passed along the stretch of road that swooped past the various utility buildings.

She knew Joan was taking her nap, so she slowed down, mindful not to make any unnecessary noise which might disturb her. As she tiptoed past the door, she could hear sobs coming from within the room. The sounds caused Victoria to stop in her tracks, for these were no ordinary sobs, not the gentle crying of a woman who was overtired or who was suffering over some petty quarrel.

The sounds were heart rending, pathetic and lonesome, filled with despair and hopelessness. The sounds tore at Victoria's heart, squeezing every last drop of blood from it, as she stared helplessly at the closed door. What was she to do? she wondered, unaware that she was biting at her knuckles. Teddy wasn't on the premises, she had seen him drive off earlier, so that meant Joan was alone in her room. Perhaps ill? Perhaps hurt? No, those weren't the cries of a woman hurt physically.

They were the cries of a woman who was suffering heartbreak! But should she interfere? she wondered nervously as the sounds continued, stabbing at the very core of her own heartbreak.

Then she knocked at the door. A soft tap at first, then a louder tap, until she was literally banging at the door, her anxiety mounting until at last she flung the door wide open to catch Joan desperately trying to mop the tears from her face. The room was almost in total darkness even though it was mid-afternoon. Joan had drawn all the shades and was sitting in her chair in the middle of the room, blinking at the light from the corridor and at Victoria standing there.

She looked so miserable sitting there all alone, so tiny and frail and helpless, that Victoria flew across to her and impulsively knelt by her side, grabbing the little body to her, rocking her to and fro while she gently smoothed back Joan's hair.

After several minutes when Victoria sensed that Joan was calmer, she got up and opened the shades, and instantly the room became more cheerful. Going back to Joan, she took her hands in her own and said gently. 'It helps to talk, you know. I probably won't be much good at offering advice, so I won't try, but I do have a sympathetic ear if you'd like to give it a try.'

'I feel I can talk to you,' Joan answered, a small smile appearing on her lips, 'and I'm glad you're here—I really am.' She wheeled her chair over to the window. 'It's Teddy,' she confessed at last. 'He's been so unhappy lately, but he won't tell me why.' She swung her chair around to face Victoria. 'I know you and Teddy don't . . . exactly like each other, I've seen it on your faces and I've even heard Teddy say rude . . . belligerent things to you. I . . . I've questioned him on his ridiculously unfair attitude towards you and I've even suggested we pay you for all the work you've done. Really, I honestly can't say how we would have managed without you,' she told Victoria, and there was no mistaking the sincerity in her voice as she gazed sadly across the room at the fair-haired girl perched on the edge of the bed.

Victoria watched her, her own heart twisting painfully in her chest, wanting desperately to explain to Joan the reasons behind Teddy's behaviour because she sensed that Joan felt Teddy's unhappiness was somehow direct-ly related to her and she was appealing to Victoria for an explanation—an explanation that Victoria was not at liberty to divulge, even though the matter had now been put right.

When the explanation that Joan was seeking didn't come, she sighed and wheeled her chair closer to Victoria, obviously concluding that this lovely girl who had been so kind and helpful towards her had merely been an innocent victim of her husband's unreasonable be-haviour. 'We've had this place for five years now,' she said, a faint tremor in her voice, 'and until recently

Teddy has loved it, we both have. He's worked so hard on it,' she sighed, remembering. 'It was half the size it is now when first we bought it and so run down you wouldn't believe the stories,' she half laughed. 'But Teddy worked night and day getting the place restored, building the guest cottages, making it what it is today,' she finished proudly.

'It is . . . beautiful,' agreed Victoria, thinking that of all the punishments Nicholas had dished out to her, none could compare with this.

'Yes,' replied Joan, pleased that Victoria should agree. 'When we first decided to buy the place, people told us it was a worthless piece of real estate, but property values have risen so dramatically during the past five years that apparently it's now worth a fortune. Teddy has always felt that if anything should ever happen to him, I wouldn't be dependent on relatives to look after me, that I would always have the security and independence of having my own place. You see,' she explained, brushing a tear from her eye, 'he's never stopped blaming himself for the accident—for this,' she said, looking miserably down at the blanket covering her little legs, 'even though it wasn't his fault. The police told us afterwards that it was only Teddy's skilful hand-ling of our car that prevented us from both being killed when the lorry sideswiped us, almost forcing us over a sixty-metre embankment. But . . . but when Teddy found out I would be crippled, it tore him to pieces, almost destroyed him, until he found this place and built it up. You see,' she said softly, her eyes filling with pride and love, 'he did it for me.'

And now he thinks I've taken if from you, thought Victoria, her eyes almost black with anguish, and her face twisted with pain as she thought of the misery and heartache she had caused, and all for a few more dollars in the Webster account! No wonder Nicholas hated her, she thought grimly, remembering all the truths he had told her about the Webster Corporation, truths which up until now she hadn't believed.

But now all the conversations which she had half listened to as she was growing up sky-rocketed into her brain. She hadn't understood then, but she understood now. The Webster Corporation fed on people like the Harringtons—the little people, the weak and the vulnerable, but also the very brave.

She took a long look at Joan. Joan was one of the brave people, and Teddy . . . ? Perhaps he was the bravest of all, because he had never given up, would never give up, because his love and devotion for his wife would never allow it. Even if she had taken their property she had no doubt he would have found another . . . and started over again.

Victoria looked up to find Nicholas standing by the door, an indefinable expression on his face as he looked from Joan to herself. How long had he been standing there, she wondered, and what must he be thinking? It came as a shock to her that she no longer cared, that she deserved his contempt and more, much more. She deserved his hatred, for she had tried, no matter how innocent her actions had been, to destroy his friends.

'Well, well, well,' drawled Nicholas, studying her as she rose slowly to her feet. 'I'm glad to see you've favoured at least one of us with the courtesy of saying goodbye!'

He strode over to Joan, lifting her chin to examine her face. 'You've been crying, little sister,' he said softly, straightening to cast Victoria a withering glance.

'Oh, Nicholas, really!' intercepted Joan. 'Stop behaving as though Victoria made me cry! I . . . I was just having a fit of the blues, that's all, and Victoria's been comforting me.' She gave a shaky little laugh. 'I've probably bored her to tears,' she said, looking fondly across at Victoria, 'and you must forgive Nicholas,' she added, giving him a piercing glance. 'He can be too protective at times.'

Victoria stared at them both. *His sister*, he had said! How had she never connected the resemblance? The same dark hair, the same black eyes, not to mention all the little mannerisms that ran through a family, making the unit unique. His sister! No wonder his hatred for herself had been so profound! What brother wouldn't hate somebody who had threatened his sister, especially a sister with all of Joan's redeeming qualities? Why hadn't he told her back at the shack? It wouldn't have come as a shock as it did now.

'Victoria, please don't look so tragic,' continued Joan, concern now in her voice. 'Nicholas knows you didn't make me cry, for goodness' sake.'

'I . . . I . . .' spluttered Victoria, looking helplessly at them both. 'It's just that I didn't know—I mean, Nicholas never told me you were brother and sister. It's come as a surprise, that's all,' she finished lamely.

'Oh, I'm sorry,' apologised Joan, bewildered. 'I thought you knew all along, that Nicholas must have told you.' She cast her brother a questioning glance, but one look at the dark, handsome face forbade any direct questioning. She turned back to Victoria, obviously puzzled now. 'But I didn't know you were leaving,' she said, distressed. 'Not so soon, anyway,' she sighed. 'It's been lovely having you here.'

'I—I've enjoyed it,' said Victoria, twisting at the hanky she had used to wipe away Joan's tears, not daring to look at either of them as she fought to hold back the painful lump in her throat. 'But I'm no longer needed here,' she managed finally, a wistful expression on her face. 'You only have a few guests left and . . . and . . .'

'Silly!' laughed Joan, wheeling her chair closer. 'I wasn't referring to the work you've done, although how you kept up that pace, I'll never know. And the way you've handled Penelope . . . that was a stroke of genius, making her the social convenor. I've never seen her happier, and she's asked Teddy for a full-time job.' She smiled. 'Can you imagine Penelope working for a living?' she asked, the smile turning into a grin. 'But I rather suspect David, our new tour guide, has something to do with her decision.' She reached up to touch Victoria's hand, her voice ringing with sincerity as she said, 'It's your company I'll miss. We seem to understand each other and I can talk to you . . . as an equal.' She dabbed at her eyes and Nicholas came to stand beside her, a protective hand resting lightly on her shoulder, but only Victoria could see the contempt in his eyes as he said, 'Now, Joan, we mustn't detain Victoria any longer than necessary. She's a high-powered business lady, you know,' he added curtly, sardonically. 'Her desk must be covered with files and briefs . . . new prospects!'

Joan caught the tone in his voice and saw the resulting flush on Victoria's face, but Nicholas didn't allow her time for comment. 'Well, Miss Webster, your bags are packed and just outside the door.'

Dismissed! 'Yes, I'll go now, but . . . but . . .'

'Yes?' he demanded, a distinct gleam of suspicion in his black eyes.

'Nothing,' she answered finally, managing a smile as she turned to Joan. 'I'm sure everything will work out for you,' she suggested gently, 'and if you wouldn't mind, perhaps we could keep in touch through the post.'

'I'd like that,' agreed Joan happily. 'And maybe next

year you'll decide to spend your holidays with us again,' she supplied hopefully.

Outside the door, Victoria grabbed her small suitcase and tucked her briefcase under her arm, her tears almost blinding her as she hurried down the corridor to the main lobby. Fortunately the lobby was empty, so she wasn't forced to endure any curious glances as she fumbled through the telephone directory, wildly searching for a taxi number to ring. With trembling fingers she managed to dial a number, only to receive a signal telling her she had misdialled. She flicked frantically at the receiver to clear the line to dial again, when a strong brown hand closed over her own and the phone was taken from her.

'I'll drive you to the airport,' said Nicholas, his voice sharp and edged with fury. 'I'd never hear the end of it if Joan found out that our esteemed "guest" had to make her own way to the airport.'

'No!' she cried, turning abruptly away from him as she wiped at her eyes. 'No . . . I would prefer to go on my own. I . . . I don't want you to drive me, I . . . I don't want to spend all that time alone with you in the jeep. I couldn't b-bear it,' she sobbed helplessly, her hands covering her face.

'Stop blubbering like a baby!' Nicholas bit out in disgust, grabbing her shoulders and shaking her. 'You're not the victim here, so stop pretending.' He held her at arm's length. 'God, you're a mess! Go and wash your face—and don't try anything funny, because I'll be right outside the door.'

He led her to the small public Ladies', opening the door for her. Two minutes later she emerged, looking not much better than she had before, but the brief interlude had given her the breather she needed.

Nicholas eyed her critically and she bravely returned his gaze, her eyes large and solemn in her face. 'I'm ready,' she announced stiffly, before turning to march like a small wooden soldier towards the door. But once more he grabbed her shoulders, swinging her roughly around to face him. His eyes roamed her face and she had the eerie sensation that he was memorising her features.

'Why were you sneaking off?' he asked roughly. 'I found that twit Graeme Muir waiting for you outside the entrance. I questioned him and he said he was taking you to the airport.'

'I wasn't sneaking off,' she denied shakily, 'and I don't see what right you had sending him away. He's a very nice young man and I'm sure he didn't appreciate your bullying him.'

He laughed, the sound not altogether unpleasant. 'I told him you'd changed your mind, that you'd decided not to leave today. I don't think that was bullying him.'

'Even so, you interfered where you had no right, and now you've made me miss my plane and I'll probably have to wait hours before I can board another!'

'Not so,' he said, puzzling her by his tone. 'I've checked the airport and most planes south are flying on schedule, that's why I couldn't understand your sudden need to leave without wishing any of us a *fond* farewell.'

'You love twisting that knife deeper and deeper into my back,' she said with a sigh, 'and I know you won't allow me a moment's peace until I admit I was planning on leaving without saying goodbye.' She peeped up at him through the thick veil of her lashes. 'But I haven't escaped after all,' she told him with a catch in her voice. 'I'm still here to listen to . . . to how much you hate me!'

His fingers bit into the soft flesh of her shoulders, causing her to wince and cry out with the sudden pain. 'Listen to me, Victoria,' he rasped, his hand leaving her shoulder to cup her chin, forcing her head upward, as he lowered his own to look deeply into her eyes. 'I don't hate you, I love you!'

He took his hand away from her chin, to slide it restlessly through his hair, his eyes never leaving her face. 'My God, Victoria,' he half-whispered, his voice raw with emotion as he studied her, the pain in his own eyes reflected in hers. 'I thought I'd lost you . . . these past two weeks, you were so cold, so uncaring, with that cute little nose of yours stuck high in the air. If you only knew how close I came to grabbing you and thrashing you! I wanted to make violent love to you, to have you lying pale and lifeless in my arms, to keep you there, eternally exhausted and unable to carry on with those blasted chores you seemed forever occupied with.' Suddenly he smiled, his teeth flashing white against the dark hue of his skin. 'Tell me, wench,' he drawled, 'doesn't that sound like the actions of a man who's crazy in love with his woman?'

'I'm not certain,' Victoria owned, lowering her eyes. 'You could be just making fun of me, trying to hurt me some more. You can be very cruel, you know, Nicholas,' she added with an indignant sniff.

He chuckled, gently drawing her to him. 'I've never met anyone like you,' he said softly, his lips nuzzling one pink little ear. 'I don't just love you, I adore you. You've wriggled your way into my heart and there's no way in the world you're going to wriggle out of it. You're mine, I've waited for you and it's not going to do you any good to protest about it. So stop fidgeting,' he commanded gruffly, 'and put your arms around me. Tell me you love me and make it convincing.'

She slipped her arms around his waist and laid her cheek against his heart. 'I love you, Nicholas,' she whispered brokenly, 'but for us there could be no future.'

He held her away from him, his eyes searching for an explanation.

She shook her head, lowering her eyes to avoid the fierceness of his own as he continued to study her. 'It wouldn't work,' she managed at last. 'You shouldn't have interfered . . . you should have let me catch that plane.'

'You said you loved me and I believe you do. You know I love you, so what's the problem?'

'You don't trust me,' she said simply, a small, sad smile on her face. 'Without trust, love soon crumbles.'

'More Webster philosophy?' he asked derisively.

Her shoulders sagged helplessly. 'Yes,' she answered gently, bending to pick up her cases. 'I am a Webster, after all, and nothing can change that fact . . . no matter how much you mock me.' She started towards the door, head held high and proud. 'Don't worry about driving me to the airport,' she called over her shoulder. 'I'll walk.'

'Twenty miles?' asked Nicholas with amusement as he stepped in front of her to swing open the doors.

'Yes,' she answered curtly, moving through the doors with great dignity. 'I desperately need the fresh air. Snobs always seem to suck all the oxygen from a room, making it rather stuffy and difficult to breathe.'

'Tell you what,' he said, wrestling the cases from her clenched fingers, 'you get in the jeep and I'll open all the windows. That way we'll both be able to recover.'

Victoria stopped in her tracks. 'Are you accusing me of being a snob?' she asked incredulously.

'Baby,' he drawled, 'who do you think I've been taking my lessons from?'

'Probably from the scrolls your ancestors wrote when they first invented the club!' she returned haughtily, small chin thrust defiantly forward.

He roared with laughter while she stood facing him, fighting an almost overwhelming desire to kick him, when he put his arm around her shoulder and led her to the jeep. 'It's time I took you in hand and taught you a few manners,' he told her, opening the door and tossing in her cases before helping her in. Once inside himself, he glanced across at her, smiling at her prim, rigid attitude. 'For a start,' he went on, 'why have you been wearing your hair up and tucked together with those blasted pins?'

'Not that it's any of your business,' she declared, 'but if you must know, it suits my present mood.'

'I don't like it!'

'I don't care!'

Nicholas chuckled and started the jeep, backing out of the driveway with a reckless speed. 'Your lessons are way overdue,' he told her smugly, 'but I blame myself for your neglect . . . a fact I'll try hard to remember when I'm bringing you to heel!'

When he ignored the turn to the airport, Victoria became alarmed. 'Where are you taking me?' she demanded, grabbing at his arm.

He shrugged her off, a ruthless smile on his face as his eyes gleamed wickedly down at her. 'A small detour, little one, before I take you to the Estate. They're expecting us.'

'B-But the airport . . . my plane . . .'

'Forget both,' he interrupted. 'I have. Besides, you would like to see where I work, wouldn't you?'

'Yes, of course, but . . .'

'Then be quiet,' he ordered gruffly. 'The roads are still in pretty poor shape and I need to concentrate.'

Even though the route was different, Victoria knew long before they arrived at the shack that this was where he was taking her. Everything was as they left it, quiet and peaceful. The chickens were gone from their pen, she saw, and she couldn't help but miss them. They had been part of her dream world.

He helped her down from the jeep, taking her small hand in his large one as he led her towards the shack. She hung back, reluctant to go inside, knowing what was sure to follow!

'Come,' he said, beckoning to her from the open door.

'No,' she answered stoutly, backing away from him. 'You tricked me into coming here, but you won't force me to do . . . anything else!'

Nicholas laughed softly, reaching out a long arm to drag her inside. 'The first thing we do is this,' he said, reaching for and finding all the pins that were holding her hair in place, tossing them carelessly aside as her hair fell in graceful lengths down her back and across her shoulders.

'Next we do this.' Down came the zipper of her pretty pink dress. He slipped it from her shoulders and let it fall to the floor.

'Now this.' He unfastened her bra and it joined her dress, leaving her naked in front of him except for her panties. She saw the passion in his eyes as he gazed hungrily at her breasts, causing her to feel both proud and ashamed of the desire she knew she created in him. She bowed her head and her hair swung forward, covering her breasts. He pulled her to him, crushing her against the smooth hard wall of his chest. She struggled, but Nicholas captured both her hands in one of his, forcing them behind her back, before his mouth came down, cruel and hard, on her own, while his free hand roughly caressed the sweet tenderness of her breast. Instantly she felt herself growing limp in his arms as her body strained towards him, every nerve awake, rioting, clamouring for release.

She felt him pick her up and carry her to the cot, and it was as though she was floating on a great tidal wave. He leaned over her to kiss her gently, before he began unbuttoning his shirt. She reached out to stroke his chest, to run her fingers lovingly across his face, and he groaned, moving next to her, his hands exploring every inch of her body, his mouth hot and insistent, nuzzling the rosy tips of her breasts. Victoria moved against him, unaware of how sensuous her body was, until at last, both of them consumed by their own passion, they reached a shattering climax.

Afterwards she lay in his arms, basking in the security and protection of his love. Nicholas leaned over her propped up on one elbow, tenderly stroking her hair. 'The lengths I must go to,' he pretended to sigh, 'to make you realise how much you love me!'

She chuckled happily, her eyes glowing with love and pride as she gazed up at him. 'I suppose this means I won't be catching that plane?'

'It does indeed,' he confirmed, kissing the tip of her nose.

'And I suppose you'll be rushing me into marriage, before I have a chance to change my mind?'

'That too,' he acknowledged, kissing the little dimple by the side of her mouth.

'Then I suppose we'd better get dressed, so you can introduce me to your boss. I wonder if he'll like me?'

'He'll adore you,' he murmured, kissing the hollow of her throat.

'Good! Then maybe he'll give you a raise!'

'Money-grabbing female!' Nicholas moaned, rising from the cot to fetch her clothes.

Victoria wanted the drive to continue for ever, it was so wonderful to have him close without anyone near to come between them, or distract any of his attention away from her. The scenery changed, the flatness giving way to small undulating hills that were rich and green, forming a lush background of plush-looking velvet for the thousands of wildflowers that sprinkled gaily across the plateaux. In the distance was the Pacific Ocean, its turquoise waters lapping gently against the startling purity of the clean white sands.

They drove through an arched gateway announcing that this was PACIFIC ESTATE, and instantly she became nervous, knowing she was about to meet Nicholas' employer. Just inside the huge gates, he stopped the jeep so they could better view the horses that were grazing in a series of excellent paddocks. 'Look over there,' he pointed.

But she had already seen him. 'Dynamite!' she shouted, jumping from the jeep to lean across the fence, her eyes sparkling with a kind of gleeful joy. 'You old rogue!' she called out to him. 'How long have you been here?'

'I thought you didn't like him,' teased Nicholas, joining her while he too leaned over the rail.

'I don't like him,' she lied, grinning. 'Just look at him!' she laughed, pointing. 'That's who you've been taking your lessons from! What a *snob* he is, looking down his long nose at his mates, quietly rebuking them—so arrogant, so pompous! It's a pity, really, that you don't own him, you're both so much alike.'

'Come on, little one,' laughed Nicholas, holding her close. 'All this flattery will surely turn my head. Let's get up to the house, so I can show you off.'

When they reached the house Victoria stared in amazement at the white, two-storey mansion. All she could think of when she saw it was that it was the same home she had seen in the old movie *Gone with the Wind*.

'Wow!' she gasped. 'Your employer . . . he must be a millionaire!'

Nicholas shrugged. 'So people say.'

Then people were swarming from the house, arms outstretched to greet them both, Nicholas returning their hugs and kisses and then passing them on to Victoria, who shyly allowed herself to be embraced and petted, her confusion mounting with every second. Was *this* how people in Queensland greeted their employees? she was shocked into wondering.

The explanation came after dinner, a sumptuous meal of roast lamb, sweet potatoes, hordes of vegetables and a choice of salads, ending with a tart-sweet lemon pie. Nicholas occupied the seat at the head of the table, carving the meat and chatting away quite as though he owned the place. Which he did!

'Great-Grandfather built this place when he was still a young man and it now serves mainly as a meeting place for the Sangster clan whenever they feel in need of a holiday, or when they suspect something's in the air.' He smiled down at her as they strolled through the gardens, his arm draped protectively across her small shoulders. 'I'm afraid we'll have to put up with them until after the wedding, if that's all right with you.'

She smiled happily. 'I wouldn't mind having them here all the time, they all seem such fun. Especially your aunt Nell! She's a riot.'

Nicholas chuckled. 'I'm glad you like her. She's eighty years old and her mind is still as sharp as a razor. She's a permanent resident, so your wish has been taken care of. Her main interest in the Sangster Corporation is race-horses, that's why she was going out of her way to dazzle you with her knowledge of horses,' he laughed. 'She figures you must be pretty up on the subject if you were able to ride Dynamite.'

But Victoria hadn't heard anything beyond Sangster Corporation! 'You . . . you're a corporation?' she gasped, her heart thumping in wild disorder. 'You're a corporation!' she repeated once more, her eyes wide with incredulous disbelief. 'How *dare* you be a corporation,' she fumed angrily, 'when you've done nothing but harass me about the Webster Corporation!'

'Ah, but we're a corporation with a difference,' he told her, unperturbed by her anger. 'We use our own money for our investments, and if it ever happens that we invest unwisely, then it's only ourselves that we hurt.'

'But what about Joan and Teddy?' asked Victoria then. 'Surely they've a right to some of this?' Her arm swept the beautiful landscaped gardens, the oversized swimming pool, the tennis courts, the stables and the grand old colonial mansion.

'Joan receives her share of the estate, which she reinvests, but Teddy won't take any of it for himself. You heard what Joan said. Teddy wants to do it on his own, and every man has the right to create his own empire, a right which must be respected.'

'Yes, but it doesn't seem fair to see them struggling . . .'

'He was doing fine until your father got his hooks into him,' Nicholas interrupted gently. 'But you're right, it isn't fair, and if I hadn't been in Europe and the States it wouldn't have taken long to figure something was up, and if Teddy had kept Joan informed she could have received help from the family. As it was . . .'

'Excuse me, Mr Sangster,' a young maid approached them, 'there's a telephone call for you,' she said, smiling shyly at Victoria.

'Thank you, Susan, I'll take it by the pool,' said Nicholas, excusing himself to Victoria as he strode off, tall and straight and self-assured, equally at home in a shack or a mansion, born into power without corruption. It was hard to believe that such a man could love her, she thought, as she watched him pick up the phone before she turned to wander thoughtfully through the scented flowerbeds. What would his family think when they learned what she had done to Teddy and Joan? she kept thinking, because sooner or later the truth would come out, as it always did, and she would forever feel a culprit.

She didn't hear him approach her, so when he turned her gently round to face him, he was struck by the sadness in her eyes, just as she was struck by the almost blinding love and pride that shone from his. He drew her close, his arms cradling her protectively against his chest, and she knew instinctively that he understood what her thoughts had been.

'That was Teddy on the phone,' he murmured huskily against her hair. 'He just got home and went straight to his office and found a very important envelope waiting for him on his desk. It seems the envelope contained the contract he'd signed . . . ripped and torn and quite useless.'

A great, heartbroken sob tore from her throat. 'What good does it do now, after I've caused them so much misery?' she sobbed, 'and what about Joan . . . when sh-she finds out how I h-hurt her husband, she'll h-hate me!'

'Shhh,' he soothed her, tenderly stroking her hair. 'Joan already knows, and she feels Teddy has learned a hard-earned lesson by keeping everything to himself. They're on their way here now and bringing the cheque you gave him as part settlement.'

'I want them to have it,' Victoria said firmly. 'It's little enough compensation for the exorbitant interest rates they were forced to pay, not to mention the worry I caused them.'

'And if they refuse?' he asked, smiling down at her upturned face, all the love and tenderness she so badly needed there in his eyes for her to see.

'They won't,' she said softly, her eyes glowing with love as she gazed up at him. 'I'll be their silent partner.'

'Very silent, my little love, my own sweet corporate lady!' Nicholas said huskily as his lips covered hers, drowning out all sound and making everything very silent indeed!

Only the flowers were there to see . . . and to whisper about their love.

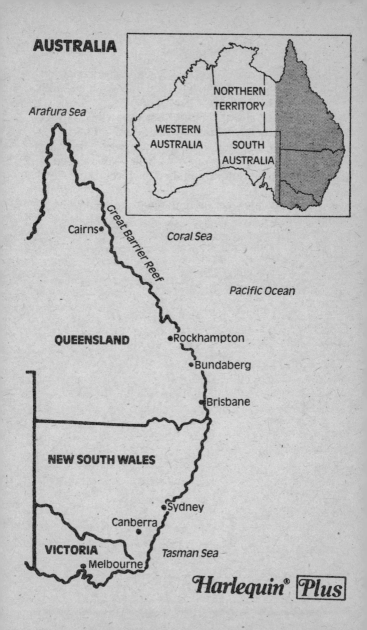

Great old favorites...
Harlequin Classic Library

The **HARLEQUIN CLASSIC LIBRARY**
is offering some of the best in romance fiction—
great old classics from our early publishing lists.

Complete and mail this coupon today!

Harlequin Reader Service

In U.S.A. P.O. Box 52040
Phoenix, AZ 85072-2040

In Canada 649 Ontario Street
Stratford, Ontario N5A 6W2

Please send me the following novels from the Harlequin Classic Library. I am enclosing my chèque or money order for $1.50 for each novel ordered, plus 75¢ to cover postage and handling. If I order all nine titles at one time, I will receive a FREE book, *Village Doctor*, by Lucy Agnes Hancock.

☐ 136 **Love Is My Reason** (#494)
Mary Burchell

☐ 137 **This Merry Bond** (#583)
Sara Seale

☐ 138 **The Happy Enterprise** (#487)
Eleanor Farnes

☐ 139 **The Primrose Bride** (#988)
Kathryn Blair

☐ 140 **My Heart Has Wings** (#483)
Elizabeth Hoy

☐ 141 **Master of Hearts** (#1047)
Averil Ives

☐ 142 **The Enchanted Trap** (#951)
Kate Starr

☐ 143 **The Garden of Don José** (#928)
Rose Burghley

☐ 144 **Flamingoes on the Lake** (#976)
Isobel Chace

Number of novels checked @ $1.50 each =	$	
N.Y. and Ariz. residents add appropriate sales tax	$	
Postage and handling	$	.75
	TOTAL $	

I enclose _____
(Please send check or money order. We cannot be responsible for cash sent through the mail.)

Prices subject to change without notice.

Name _____
(Please Print)

Address _____
(Apt. no.)

City _____

State/Prov. _____ Zip/Postal Code _____

Offer expires November 30, 1984   CL-116   40556000000